Vera,
Best wishes,
Gaye Pollinger

Gayse Pollinger

TATE PUBLISHING
AND ENTERPRISES, LLC

The Persnickety Witch of Fiddyment Creek
Copyright © 2015 by Gaye Pollinger. All rights reserved.

No part of this publication may be reproduced, stored in a retrieval system or transmitted in any way by any means, electronic, mechanical, photocopy, recording or otherwise without the prior permission of the author except as provided by USA copyright law.

This novel is a work of fiction. Names, descriptions, entities, and incidents included in the story are products of the author's imagination. Any resemblance to actual persons, events, and entities is entirely coincidental.

The opinions expressed by the author are not necessarily those of Tate Publishing, LLC.

Published by Tate Publishing & Enterprises, LLC
127 E. Trade Center Terrace | Mustang, Oklahoma 73064 USA
1.888.361.9473 | www.tatepublishing.com

Tate Publishing is committed to excellence in the publishing industry. The company reflects the philosophy established by the founders, based on Psalm 68:11,
"The Lord gave the word and great was the company of those who published it."

Book design copyright © 2015 by Tate Publishing, LLC. All rights reserved.
Cover design by Nino Carlo Suico
Interior design by Manolito Bastasa

Published in the United States of America

ISBN: 978-1-63449-992-7
Fiction / General
15.01.12

For my son, Jeremy, who left Southern California and moved with me to Illinois when he wasn't crazy about the idea. He came along for the ride and conceptualized this story. Without him there would be no persnickety witch. Deet-do (thank you)!

Acknowledgements

After living away from Joliet, Illinois, for thirty-something years, I decided to return to my roots. I had lived in Chicago's northwest suburbs, Southern Illinois, West Africa, and Southern California; I missed family and friends. And the glorious colors of autumn.

Jeremy, my son, moved with me and we were out exploring one day. The area had changed, grown, added roads and highways, and there were thriving communities where farms and their crops once stood. One day, we were driving south on newly-opened 355, and I spied a sign in big black letters that said *Fiddyment Creek.* I repeated the words a couple of times and liked the way they rolled off my tongue. He suggested that I write about it. "What on earth would I write?" I asked. "I don't know, Mom," he answered. "How about the persnickety witch of Fiddyment Creek?" My imagination immediately began to toss around several ideas to create the story of a little girl, an older woman, and a terrible misunderstanding.

Two trusted friends were my go-to readers, and I would e-mail them new pages as they were written. I could count on them to ask questions and give me critiques, ideas, suggestions, and encouragement. They never seemed to tire; they always wanted more.

I became curious about general stores and my friend, Cathy, went with me on a field trip to a nearby small town that still has an operating general store. I watched video footage of an actual Fiddyment Creek flood; I did research on tornadoes and equine therapy; I worked with a stroke victim and helped her speak again; and I talked to a California friend who had been adopted as an adult.

I have reached the point in this wonderful journey to thank those who were my encouragers and enthusiastic assistants in the writing of PWOFC. First, thank you, God, for giving me the gift of creativity and for working out the myriad details. You promised to take care of me—and you always have. I was very aware of your presence and the day-to-day miracles I experienced. Thanks to eagle-eye Joyce Gilmour who did the preliminary copy editing, helped me work out the bugs, became my friend, and was only a phone call away. Huge thanks to Tate Publishing and all of the staff who worked on this project with patience and understanding. In no particular order, a ginormous boatload of humble, heartfelt thanks goes to Jeremy Pollinger, Cathy Reinhardt, Linda Koy, Amy Yago, Sue Lopez, Kathy Sanchez, Edie Libby, Dora Komaromi, Dianne Erman, John David Webster, Joann Adams, Glenn Franz, Carol Bachman, Jim Vandenburg, Kimberly Motley, Jim Harmon, Dorothy Rung, the ladies in my book club aka Biblio Babes, June Rendleman, Bob Gonda, Sharon Nelson, Katy Brand, Jaye Ahoyt, Gail Rendleman, Joel Munyon, Jenni Snider, my cousin Sherry Ross (who died from ALS before the story was completed), Rick Schultz, Pamela Wiggins Campbell, Patricia Wiggs, Paz Beegle (my aunt and cheerleader who passed away before she could see the finished product), Colette Ehresman, Kathy and Martin Ivec, Sandi and Alan Von Behren, and others I may have forgotten. Please receive my thanks, appreciation, gratitude, love, and a big ol' bear hug.

Chapter 1

The children scurried to find a spot on the floor mat as close to me as possible. They sat cross-legged, with hands folded in their laps. A foggy mist slowly wrapped itself around the children. They weren't afraid of the mysteriousness. As they settled, I looked each child in the eye. I knew I had their attention, so I began telling the story, "Good morning to you, boys and girls. My name is Miss Lucy and I was just wondering…have you ever heard of the persnickety witch?" I paused and looked at each child. "She wears a funny straw hat and rides a faded red bicycle. Everyone has a story. Even you." I directed my attention toward a wide-eyed boy. "This morning I'd like to tell you her story. *Her* story is amazing, incredible, and hard to believe. She's quite a character and very charming if you get to know her. She notices *every* single thing, right down to the scabby scratch on your knee or the finest details of a flower petal growing alongside Fiddyment Creek, which bubbles and gurgles merrily on its way toward the river. That's what makes her persnickety.

"If you haven't seen her or don't know who she is, let me help you picture her in your mind's eye. Close your eyes so you can see her. Are your eyes closed? I'm not sure of her age, but she's quite tall and slender. She puts her long, grayish-white hair up off her neck and secures it with hairpins, but strands of it sometimes escape out from under her straw hat. She wears a dress covered up by a bibbed and pocketed apron, and she wears an old pair of red PF Flyers on her feet. She tucks some petals of lavender into a sachet and wears it with a ribbon around her neck. If you get close enough, you can smell the lavender. She has a gently wrinkled face, which appears to be soft. Wire-rimmed glasses that perch at the end of her nose are usually ready to fall off, and she has very sparkly, deep blue eyes, one has a teeny-tiny spot with a glimmer of gold.

When I was much younger—about the same age as you—I heard that she was picky, choosy, finicky, feisty, and fussy. Somehow, sometime, little children overheard adults call her the persnickety witch. Why? She didn't look anything at all like a witch. A witch! But I'm afraid that name stuck.

Have you ever seen where she lives? Well, my goodness, each time I go past, I notice something new to admire. It's nothing at all like where you'd think a witch would live.

There's absolutely whatsoever no sign of a cauldron. But there are lacey curtains at the windows, two creaking rocking chairs on the front porch, and wind chimes—both large and small—hanging from carved wooden figures or animals attached to cup hooks on the porch rafters. A huge asparagus fern and an enormous Boston fern spill in long waves over the sides of hanging baskets. The only thing witchy about her that I've noticed is Chester, her gorgeous black cat with huge green eyes. Chester likes to park himself on one of the rockers for a catnap and every so often he *s-t-r-e-t-c-h-e-s* lazily. She loves beautiful lavender bushes and colorful flowers. She grows all sorts of flowers in practically anything—an old boot, a copper teapot, a dented-in bucket, a wooden crate. Look around in your mind. You'll see. The sunflowers out back are especially tall this summer—almost as tall as the roof of the cottage. A flurry of deep purple morning glories encircle the railings of the four, no, five stairs climbing to the porch; a sweet-smelling peony bush heavy with pinkish-white blossoms complete with ants scurrying from blossom to blossom stands guard at the bottom of the wooden stairs. A smooth stone pathway meanders to the front, the side, and around the back of the cottage. A white picket fence surrounds the yard. Roses grow at the front of the house on either side of the picket gate in a kaleidoscope of colors, and their fragrance is almost overwhelming. Hummingbirds, bumblebees, and butterflies stay in the yard and dart from flower to flower. To the right of the house is a vegetable garden, and big, red, beefy tomatoes are almost, but not quite, ready to pluck from the vine.

"So, there you have it. That describes the woman known as the persnickety witch. Thanks for com—"

The children made groans and sounds of complaint.

"More? You want more? Are you ready for her story? Would you like to know about the persnickety witch of Fiddyment Creek?"

I paused and waited for the children to respond. They all bobbed their heads up and down. Some whispered "Yes," but they all sat quietly, and so I continued with the story.

Early each morning, the persnickety witch plopped a beaten-up old straw hat onto her gray hair, climbed onto her old faded red Schwinn bicycle, rode past driveways and people out walking their dogs, and dodged newspapers tossed onto the sidewalk by the paperboy, occasionally slowing, but never coming to a complete stop. One morning she was in a hurry. Every so often, she pressed the lever of the bicycle's bell to let everyone know she was coming. A mason jar filled with something-or-other and a small bouquet of flowers from her garden bounced in the bike's basket attached to the handlebars.

"Morning, Penel..." said the old woman as she rolled past. Her voice trailed off as she pedaled along.

"Morning..." Penelope began, but she never could remember the old woman's name. And anyway, she was halfway into the next block. "What *is* her name?" Penelope wondered aloud as she looked up from pouring water from the big metal green watering can.

The old woman was quite a sight with that old straw hat and her usual attire, and you could set your clock by her daily trips. Toddlers liked to stand by the gates of their yards and wave their chubby fingers at her. She would always grin real big and wave back. Children that age hadn't learned yet to be mean or cruel.

It's interesting that nobody ever thought to follow her. I did, but that comes a little later in the story. I grew up here in Fiddyment and was raised by an aunt who arrived soon after my mother died and my father took off to parts unknown. Now I am a mother with a daughter, Cathy, who is in the third grade and loves to learn everything about people and the world, and Jameson, one of the toddlers who enjoys watching her ride past each morning. Fiddyment is a small town where you know everybody by name; you don't have to lock your doors at night, and you walk in for a visit with a high-pitched *yoo-hoooo*, but without knocking.

"Good mor..." I yelled with a lilt to my voice as she approached. She raised her right arm into the air and flicked her wrist with fingers extended as her response. I'm sure I made a sourpuss face, but I saw that Penelope was still out, so I grabbed Jameson's short, stubby fingers and we made our way over to the next yard.

"Hey, Penelope…what's her story?" I said almost cantankerously as I nodded my head toward the diminishing figure on the bike, watching as she disappeared.

"Bring Jamie over and we'll have coffee. The boys can play while we visit," Penelope replied. Penelope's dark eyes sparkled with the thought of sharing about the persnickety witch of Fiddyment Creek. I'm sure I bristled when Penelope referred to my son as Jamie.

"Penelope, you know that his name is *Jameson*," I said, my voice low, as I rounded the fence.

Stuff like that really irritated me. After all, she had chided me when I called her Penny when we had been roommates at college. We sat in white wicker rockers on the porch that encased the entire front of the mossy green Victorian home, sipped steamy, hot coffee and dunked shortbread cookies in the dark brew while our boys, Jameson and Paulie, played with toy fire engines on the immaculate lawn below us. Paulie stood, came toward me, and held up three chubby fingers.

"I Paulie and I free year ode," he said quite understandably.

I smiled back and told him that he was a big boy.

"Hey…hey…*hey!*" he said louder each time and pulled my skirt trying to get and keep my attention. "Do you like aldergators?"

Then, quick as a flash, he was back to playing with Jameson. It was about then that Cathy came out of the front door and looked around. I spotted her and yelled.

"Hey! Cathy! We're over here!"

She bounded down the porch stairs, and I watched her skip over looking oh-so-cute in her dreamsicle-colored shorts and matching halter top. We named her Kathleen after my mother, but she wanted to be called Cathy with a C, not a K. She was the spitting image of her father with fair skin, bright green eyes framed by full lashes, and long, curly, copper-colored hair. She was full of energy from morning to night. She squatted and looked at the fire trucks, and then sat on the porch stairs pretending to be uninterested, but I knew that she was all ears.

Penelope put down her cup and fidgeted with the flowery cotton napkin in her lap before she continued, "The witch and her husband—they called him Will, but we've called her persnickety witch for so long, I don't remember her real name—came to Fiddyment a couple of years after the Depression and they built their house up on the hill above Fiddyment Creek, close to a weeping willow tree. He thought there was gold in the creek and panned for a while, but nobody ever said that he'd struck it rich. They tilled the soil and planted crops, a small garden next to the house. They had a cow or two and some chickens—and that's how they seemed to survive. Eventually, others came to Fiddyment and Will opened a general store, in that old wooden building a couple of blocks down, it's been vacant a long time, but you can still make out the initials W.O.W. up toward the roof." She nodded to the south.

"In the back corner of the store, he had a barbershop, which, as you know, is where all men like to gather whether they need to or not. Excuse me, Cathy…Jameson, Paulie, would you like a cookie?"

Penelope glanced at me for my approval and I nodded. She met them on the stairs to give them their treat and they squatted beside the trucks and munched away. Cathy counted the chocolate chips in her cookie and then nibbled on it, taking very small bites with one of her front teeth.

Penelope continued, "One spring, after a really bad, long winter, the creek was already up to the top of the banks from the snow melting, flowing swiftly, and then there was a terrible thunderstorm. You know, the kind that makes you jump out of your skin and where you can hear the angels bowling in heaven, and see gashes of lightning pierce through the sky. It must've rained nonstop for a week. The creek was beginning to spill over and flood the area. There was a cold wind blowing—the kind that could bite your skin—and it blew so hard it rained sideways. People didn't go out unless absolutely necessary. Willowby insisted that he go to the store in case someone had a need.

I could almost hear him speaking: "M'dear, I just have this feeling…if somebody needs something from the store, I must be there to help them."

But she felt uneasy about him leaving. After a moment's embrace and quick kiss on the cheek, he left. He trudged through the water and mud, opened the store's doors, and sat out on the slatted board sidewalk in front, watching and waiting. Finally, a couple of fellows came by and they went inside and started a game of chess; several others wandered in and watched. Then this wet stranger burst through the door and yelled, "*Help! Help!* My son has fallen into the creek and he got swept downstream! I couldn't reach him…I can't swim! He was holding onto a log…but…"

You could hear the panic in his voice. I can hear it now. Jameson and Paulie looked up and both of us told them to finish playing…everything was fine. Penelope was just telling a story.

"That old store down there?" Cathy asked with wonder. She had recently lost a front tooth and her tongue poked through the space when she talked. "Wow…"

Will grabbed anything that they might need—a rope, a blanket, a pickaxe, a lantern, and a shovel—and off they went following the stranger. Two of the men went to get a rowboat. Will suggested that those remaining go further downstream to see if the boy managed to get ashore, so that's what they did. As they hurried along, the distraught father told them that his son's name was Michael. They yelled his name repeatedly as they heaved weeds and reeds aside, glancing up and down Fiddyment Creek now turned into a furious river. Soon, the men with the rowboat came. Will got into the boat with them and they went farther downstream. He remarked to the men that he didn't recall ever seeing the water move so fast. It was so cold it made their teeth chatter and it chilled their bones. It was murky from the muddy bottom stirring up. They pulled the boat up onto the creek bank while tree debris, dead animals, and huge sections of a red barn floated past them.

The others arrived on foot and the men stood huddled together and prayed to Almighty God to help them. Then the unthinkable happened. A jagged bolt of lightning struck a tree across the creek, and there was a low rumble followed by a crack of thunder that sounded like a whip. Limbs and branches crashed to the ground and piled in a heap. Before they knew it, light rain began to fall and dampened their spirits even more. It was almost twilight. The sky was already darkened by pewter-colored rain-filled clouds when there was yet another splinter of lightning. This jag lit the sky a little longer. One of the men pointed to a form across the creek, huddled close to the tree that had been hit only minutes earlier.

"Michael?" the worried father whispered. Now he yelled, "Michael? Is that you?" Trancelike, he waded out to the speeding, furious creek trying to cross, and Will tried to stop him.

"Wait!" yelled Will. "Let's take the boat across!"

But the man continued. He was in chest-high water when he stumbled and disappeared below the angry creek. When he surfaced, gasping for breath, the swift current carried him away, and they could hear the terror in his voice as he yelled.

"Save my boy! Save my boy!"

Will was a strong swimmer, and he dove into the murkiness, stroked, and kicked, trying to catch up to the man. The current was powerful. The other men stood helplessly watching. They could see a big log heaving in the current, aiming itself right for Will. They yelled to warn him, but their voices were lost in the storm and the wind. The stranger went under the water at exactly the same moment that the log hit Will's head, and blood streamed all across his head and face and into his eyes and dripped into the water around him. Then Will lost consciousness and disappeared into the darkness of the raging Fiddyment Creek.

"*No!*" the men all screamed at one time, as if with one voice.

But it was too late. The remaining men managed to get the boy to the other side of the creek; they searched for Will and the stranger until darkness, and the storm stopped them. Two men perished that rainy day in April.

In the comfort of her dry home, Will's wife had been doing some mending when her head jolted and she had this gnawing in the pit of her stomach. She and Will were so in tune with each other, she just knew something had happened, and she put on a dark blue cape and started half-running, half-walking toward town. She met the distressed bunch of storm-soaked men on the muddy road, but didn't recognize the boy limping from a gash on the bottom of his foot. They all started to speak at once and she listened quietly, absorbing, processing, and watching the mud-covered and rain-soaked boy who had just endured a horrible tragedy. She didn't cry for herself that day. She would, just not now. Instead, she saved her strength for the boy, wrapped him in her cape, and took him home with her to give him some hot vegetable soup and comfort. She noticed everything about him. He was tall and gangly, and he looked to be about fifteen years old. When he was clean, he had thick brown wavy hair that needed to be cut, and his nose and cheeks were covered with freckles. His eyes were greenish-brown, his neck long, and his front teeth overlapped slightly. After a day or two, he began to talk to her. His name was Michael Morgan. He liked to read and he liked to whittle. He pulled from his pocket a whistle that he had carved in the shape of an owl. He talked about his father. He had no brothers or sisters; he never knew his mother—she had died during childbirth. Now he had no one. Will's wife told him that he could stay with her as long as he liked.

"Might as well stay here, Michael. You don't have any place else to go. You'll be like my son, Will, and I…"

Just as she finished saying that, there was a knock on the door. The itinerant pastor was there to tell them that the bodies of Will and Michael's father had been found.

Three days after the storm passed over and Fiddyment Creek's wrath ceased and the waters declined, the bodies of Will and the stranger were found floating face down side by side in a little cove about a mile from where they were last seen. The next day, there was a funeral service for both of them. The whole community came out to pay their respects to Will's widow, and to Michael, even though they didn't know him. They sat side by side on a wooden pew at the front of the little church. The men who were strangers, but were now linked forever, were buried in pine boxes next to each other in Fiddyment Cemetery.

Even before Willowby died, the woman would go sit under the weeping willow tree, write in her journal, and sometimes play her dulcimer. Now that he was gone, she would grab his weathered straw hat from the hook at the back door and plunk it on her head for her visit to the leafy, mushroom-shaped tree. She spent long hours sitting there, staring out across the bubbling water. It was there that she reminisced, cried, and grieved. She had beautiful memories of her years with Willowby, and she would move through this grief and live again.

The townfolk of Fiddyment gave her about a week to mourn, and then they started knocking on the door and telling her that they needed supplies. Was she going to open the general store? She glanced toward Michael; he nodded one time. She said that she'd be there to open up within the hour. Word spread like wildfire and by the time she and Michael got to the store, people were lined up on the raised, wooden sidewalk. The women shoppers took their time browsing and looked at new fabric that had come in just before the storm, and they offered her their condolences. Several men gathered in the barber's corner and wondered out loud who would give them a shave and a haircut and trim their nose hairs.

After a long day, the widow and Michael walked home and in his thick Southern accent, he asked her, "Can you teach me how to cut men's hair?"

So that night, she cut his hair and told him what she was doing as he watched intently, and then he practiced with the straw on the broom. The next day, the barber's corner once again opened for business.

The woman fussed over everything in the general store. She dusted shelves, rearranged canned goods, put things where they belonged, examined the huge pickle jar and the old cracker barrel, swept dust bunnies from the linoleum, stood back and looked at everything to make sure it was lined up properly, and then straightened some more. Boldly, she ordered a few unusual things from the warehouses and she gave the store a feminine touch—she even hung curtains on the windows and put a vase of flowers next to the cash register.

Now Jameson interrupted by calling out, "Mommy! Mommy, I want to go home. Mommy, can we go home?"

As you can imagine, I had a million questions I wanted to ask Penelope, but they would have to wait. Our boys had played nicely, but they were getting out of sorts and they both needed naps.

"I think I should get Jameson home. This story about the persnickety witch is so interesting. Can we continue tomorrow?" I asked tentatively.

"Sure," she answered. "The boys get along well, so come over after she waves to them in the morning."

Cathy walked silently, and I could hear her sniffing. Then she said, "Mama? Is that a true story? Why did they have to die?"

I explained to her that it was a true story about people in our town and that we all need to watch out for each other.

After Jameson's nap and him being very picky, almost persnickety, about how I cut his PB and J sandwich, I put him in a wagon and the three of us walked to town and stopped in front of the old general store. Cathy stood back on the edge of the sidewalk, looked up, and pointed to the fading initials, *W.O.W.* I stood on my tippy-toes and peered through the dirty windows. It appeared to have a little of everything—hardware, non-perishables, yard goods, fishing poles. There were still canned goods on the shelf, some mason jars, some figures of—*What is that on the counter?*—a barber's chair over there…and, oh my goodness, the chess set ready for a game.

"Interesting place, isn't it?" the woman asked me. She leaned the bike against one of the walls and stood beside me looking into a window.

Oh! She had startled me and my hands flew to my face to hide my embarrassment. I felt guilty for even being there, but she had caught me! My heart raced as I tried to think of a good answer.

"Well, yes. I was just curious about this old building."

"I bet you are," the old woman spoke under her breath. "The general store belonged to my husband and me before he passed. It used to be a gathering place. Used to be quite…" But she stopped and stared into my eyes for an uncomfortable length of time.

I held out my hand.

"My name is Lucy. Lucy Maguire. And this is my daughter, Cathy, and my son, Jameson. Children? Say hello to the nice lady."

"With a C," Cathy said impishly as she gazed up into the wizened face.

She took my hand in both of hers and looked me in the eyes. "Yes, I know who you are…I knew your mother years ago. You married Thomas, didn't you?" she asked with an inquisitive look on her face.

She turned her attention to Cathy for a moment.

"Hello, young lady with a C"—letting her know that she'd been heard—"I think you must look like your papa."

Then back to me, "Lucy, it's good to speak to you again. You have become a fine woman. Your mama would be proud." She stopped for several moments before continuing, "I'm Pearl."

There was something about the way she said her name. She cocked her head a little as if she were expecting me to recognize her.

Pearl! At last I knew her name. I no longer had to call her "persnickety witch," and I could tell Penelope tomorrow. She released my hand, waved to the kids, climbed onto her bike, said, "I'm off!" and was gone. As she rode past, I noticed the bike basket. An empty mason jar was there, but nothing else. The smell of lavender hung in the air.

The children, especially Jameson, had been so well-behaved for this outing, I felt that a treat was in order and so we stopped at Scooper Dooper for some ice cream. It was there that I decided what to do. When we got home, I hurried to the kitchen.

"Hi, Becky," I said into the telephone. "Would you be able to keep an eye on Cathy and Jameson tomorrow afternoon? Good...and could I borrow your bike?"

Chapter 2

The next morning, Pearl rode by Penelope's house in the usual manner, but slowed ever so slightly as she got to mine and yelled, "Morning, Lucy. Hi, Cathy with a C. Hey there, Jameson!" and continued on her way. Jameson clapped and giggled with glee, and Cathy jumped up and down. This old lady who fascinated everyone called my children by name!

I could sense Penelope's confused amazement, and I yelled to her.

"I'll tell you when we come over!"

I turned to watch Pearl riding down the street. I wanted to see where she went, how far she went, and exactly when she turned. Then I went inside for some blueberry muffins I had made earlier to take over to Penelope's.

"What on earth?" Penelope began as we placed everything on a small wicker table between the chairs. "How did you…?" and she stopped again, waiting for my story. She set out small plates, forks and spoons, butter, the mugs for coffee, and cream and sugar. Cookies and sweating metal glasses of Kool-Aid were waiting for Cathy and the boys when they were ready for a snack. Right now, they were busy playing in the yard. And again, Cathy found a porch step where she could see the world pass by and also listen to Penelope's story about the persnickety witch.

"You're not going to believe this, Penelope," I began excitedly. "Yesterday we all went for a walk and we stopped at the general store and I peeked in the windows. All of a sudden, she was there! I had been so interested in what I could see inside. I never even heard her ride up. She already knew who I was! And she said she had known my mother! And *then* she even told me that her name is Pearl. *Pearl!*"

"Pearl what?" asked Penelope flatly.

I deflated instantly.

"Pearl what?" I repeated almost to myself. Pickles! I still didn't know her last name! "Pearl…witch…" was all I could groan. "Just tell me more about her."

"Let's see, where was I? Oh yes." Penelope blew on the liquid before wrapping her lips around the edge of the mug for a sip of the very hot freshly percolated coffee, which delayed the storytelling even longer.

Michael attended the high school in the next town and helped out at the general store. Sometimes they would sit out on the porch and she would play her dulcimer and he played an autoharp. The sounds were beautiful and carried on the breeze into town. People would stop and listen; it was almost magical. In the evenings, he would go out to Will's woodshop and saw and hammer and who knows what else. He was good at whittling too, so eventually, figures and carved animals appeared in the store, and once he whittled an entire circus with a wooden tent and everything! Somebody liked it so much they bought it fast as a jack rabbit. He had a gift for carving, and his next project was a headboard for the wi—I mean Pearl.

Hmmmm. I wonder if she still has it? I thought to myself.

The wi—oh, honestly, Pearl had a radio at the general store and folks used to stop in there when they were out and about town to hear the news about the war and Hitler and all the terrible bombing. One day Michael was gone and Pearl told everyone that he had joined the army. My mother said that Pearl wasn't the same. After all, he was like her son, and she sent him gift boxes filled with socks and cookies and peanut brittle and she wrote lots of letters with news about Fiddyment. He was good about writing too, and he told about the places he'd been and how horrible the war was. People in the area who had boys in the war found out that their letters often didn't get through, or the letters would show up months later. There were spans of time during the war that Pearl didn't hear from Michael, and she didn't know where he was or if he was alive. People would stop into the store and ask, "Have you heard from Michael?"

"Not since the last time you asked, but I will soon" was always her polite response.

When Michael came home, he gave her something he had been working on the entire time he was gone: a carving of "The Last Supper" on a piece of wood he'd found in Germany and on the back, he etched where he was each time he worked on it.

"I would truly love to see his work," I said to nobody in particular, but mostly myself.

I must say, at least my mother often told me, that Pearl was quite a ruthless business woman and very successful. That came from her being fussy and picky, I guess. Wouldn't put up with shenanigans. Everything had to be just so. Yet she still had a sensitive side. Even taught another woman in a neighboring town how to run a business—and she did quite well too.

"Well, I enjoy these visits, but I have a doctor's appointment and we need to get ready. Tomorrow? Same time?" she asked as she stood and began to gather the dishes and put everything in a huge basket.

It was close to lunchtime and back in my kitchen, Cathy was already helping me butter the bread when I asked Jameson if he would like a grilled cheese sandwich or soup. I already knew the answer, but wanted to hear him say, "Sammich. A sammich, Mommy." I cut it into strips the way he liked. When Becky finally arrived, I couldn't wait to climb onto her bike and see if I could find where Pearl went each morning.

Pedaling down the street, I began to notice that the Village of Fiddyment had the potential to be charming, but it was stuck in time. It was typical for many of these smaller towns to have a town square. Fiddyment did, and it had been planned well. There were park benches facing the streets, lots of flowers in the spring and summer, and mums in the early fall, and mature trees gave much-needed shade in the summer. There was also a circular fountain in the middle of the square. People liked to meet there and sit on the edge of the fountain and touch the water with their fingers. Every few minutes, water streamed into the air before falling back into the basin. People often tossed in a penny or two and made a wish. Many of the surrounding buildings were built from huge pieces of limestone dug out of a nearby quarry, and the date the building opened was carved onto a cornerstone. There were still several cobblestone side streets, the sidewalks in front of the stores were elevated and had dilapidated hitching posts that had been used to accommodate horses and buggies of days long gone. Empty terra cotta containers stood beside the front doors of several businesses. It was like the proprietors just didn't care anymore. A chalkboard easel in front of Old Stone Café told passersby about the Blue Plate Special; Scooper Dooper was still popular because of its homemade ice cream and delicious concoctions; The Olde

Popcorn Shoppe was so small there was barely room to turn around and the odor of stale popcorn wafted down the street; the Bank of Fiddyment's window sign said that they were open until three o'clock; Jack's Sunoco Service Station had customers at the pumps and a car being worked on in the garage; Roxy Theater was closed until the weekend; Woolworth's Five and Dime had flip-flops and school supplies on sale.

We have the usual things to keep a town alive, I thought to myself, *but nothing to really draw people for an afternoon of fun and shopping. Hmmmm. I'd better pay attention. I think it was around here that she turned.*

How many times had I traveled this way and never seen the pathway almost hidden by the bushes and boughs of trees on either side? I turned the bike onto the secluded pathway. It was dark and cool, and continued around a bend. I decided to keep going. I looked up at the bright sky, peeking through the leaves and branches. I felt excited to be on this adventure. I could hear Fiddyment Creek, so I knew I must be riding alongside it. After another curve, the path stopped. There was nothing ahead of me but tangled climbing roses and weeds. I got off the bike, pushed gently on the foliage, and it opened—without any trouble. All of the tangled vines and growth disguised a wrought-iron fence and gate. Once inside, I thought I had discovered "The Secret Garden" that I'd read about. Instead, I realized that I was in an old cemetery and somebody had done a fine job of gardening. The next thing I noticed was that several of the oldest headstones were crumbling and were barely readable. There were others whose names I recognized—probably from overhearing people talk about Fiddyment's founding families. I stood and looked from side to side to get my bearings, and any fear I had diminished. In the middle of the cemetery was a statue of an angel keeping guard, and there were three park benches under trees. An old weather beaten greenhouse was in the far corner, and it hardly could be seen for the wildflowers growing around it. In another corner was a pump with a long handle to prime the water; hanging from the spigot was a tin cup. The cemetery was a sanctuary, and even though I was an intruder, I felt safe.

"Hello. Can I help you find something?" a familiar voice asked.

I spun around toward the sound. Sure enough. It was Pearl. She stood holding the old straw hat, and a lot of her hair had escaped from the hairpins.

"I…I…I…" I stammered. Then I sucked in a big breath and continued, "Actually I watched to see where you turned this morning. I'm just curious, Pearl. But I didn't think this was private—there's no sign that says that—and it's so peaceful in here. Is this where your husband is buried?" I answered as I asked a question of my own.

"Yes, it is, and Michael's father too," she offered. "There are two headstones here with no wording on them." She walked toward the grassy area and pointed at them with the toe of her red tennis shoe. Pansies surrounded both graves. "Willowby liked the faces on pansies," Pearl told me.

"I feel like I've known you…" I began.

Pearl nodded her head and answered, "You have. Do you drink hot tea?"

I nodded my head up and down to answer.

"Come by my place around seven o'clock this evening. I live in the white cottage on the hill. And leave the children with Thomas," she said.

"Of course. It'll be good for all of them," I said as I laughed nervously.

"Stay here as long as you like, but be sure to close the gate when you leave," Pearl told me. She slipped away, climbed onto the bike's seat, and rode down the shady pathway toward the street.

At home, I began preparing dinner. The children were watching something on television when Tom came home. I kissed him on the cheek and told him that dinner would be ready in an hour.

"We're having oven-fried chicken, corn on the cob, and mashed potatoes. Oh. And gravy. And cucumber salad. How was practice?" I asked him. "Did Frank ever learn his part?" I yelled from the dining room as I set the table.

Tom was a science teacher and the band director at Fiddyment High School. The marching band had begun rehearsals called "Three Ms"—meet, move, and march—right after school got out for the summer so they were ready for football season. Tom played the trombone and woodwind instruments in high school and college, and he worked hard at encouraging the band members to practice and show up for rehearsals. They were pretty good and had won several county and state competitions under his direction.

I could hear water in the bathroom as he took a quick shower. It had been hot today, and he had spent long hours in the sunshine. He came out of the bathroom with his hair tousled, dressed in shorts, a T-shirt, and flip-flops and looked refreshed.

"Ouch," I said when I glanced at him. "You got yourself good and burned. There's some zinc ointment in the medicine chest."

He nodded, turned around, and headed for the bathroom. He rejoined me in the kitchen and had white ointment on his nose. I mashed the potatoes, and he made the gravy. Together we put everything on the table.

"Come on, kids!" he yelled through the house. "It's time to eat, and if you don't come now, I'm going to eat everything because I'm good and hungry!"

We could hear them racing through the house, squealing, and yelling, "I wanna leg" or "I want the pulley bone."

Jameson grabbed a chicken leg and his teeth sank into the delicious crispiness. He couldn't quite handle the cob, so I cut the corn off for him.

I always liked dinnertime. We all talked about our day; occasionally, I prepared a different type of food, and the kids were good about trying it. We enjoyed teaching the kids etiquette and table manners, and there was a genuine feeling of love, family, and togetherness. Tonight, Cathy was very chatty about Pearl and the story we had been hearing from Penelope. That opened up the conversation for me to tell about the hidden pathway, the cemetery, and to ask Tom to watch the kids this evening because of my special invitation.

"But why can't I go too?" Cathy whined.

"Well, Kathleen Erin Maguire, I'm sure there will be other times that you can go, but this is very special for Mommy, and you and Jameson and I will make popcorn and watch TV together, okay?" Tom said, coming to my rescue.

Cathy knew that when we used at least two of her names, we meant business, and she settled down.

"I'll just rinse these and take care of them later," I said as I cleared the table.

"There's apple pie on the counter and vanilla ice cream in the freezer."

I climbed the stairs to our bedroom and stood in my closet, looking for something to wear.

"Did you know I used to deliver Persnick's groceries from Sitter's Store when I was in high school?" Tom asked from the bedroom doorway.

"No, you never mentioned it," I replied.

"Didn't seem important, I guess, but I sort of got to know her a little. Man! She had the greatest car…from Great Britain, I think." He turned to go back toward the living room and the kids.

I decided on a yellow sundress and thought I looked pretty nice for my visit with Pearl. I had my hair pulled back into a ponytail with a yellow ribbon at the nape. As I turned the key of Tom's pride and joy, a '55 candy apple–red T-Bird with white leather upholstery and white-walled tires, I wondered what was in store for me. It wasn't a long drive at all, just a few blocks and then up a little hill on a long gravel driveway. A bobwhite had been sitting on a split-rail fence beside the stony driveway, whistling the familiar "bob-bob-white," and flew off. My hair blew in the breeze with the top down. I turned off the ignition and began to retie the ribbon when Pearl opened the screen door and waved at me. I got out of the car and walked over toward the gate. It had bells that jangled when the gate opened and closed. The fragrance of roses penetrated my nostrils. She had seated herself on a swing and beckoned me up. I guessed that she was about sixty. She wore a blue-print dress with lace around the neck's edge; she had rolled her hair into a French twist, but still a few wisps of it escaped and gently hung beside her ears. She smelled of lavender. Chester, her black cat, lay beside her feet. He opened his green eyes and watched me as I climbed the stairs, then put his head down on his front paws and went back to sleep.

"Your flowers and garden are just lovely," I said as I got to the top stair. "You certainly have a green thumb, Pearl.

I've never seen such a healthy Boston fern! It's so big and full!" I let my fingers gently touch the pointed leaves.

"I've had that fern for many a year," Pearl said. "It just really seems to like the view from the porch. We're up here away from everything 'cept God. My, my, just look at that sunset," she said as she moved back and forward in a homemade swing. "Some of those colors we'll never see again."

I sat in a rocking chair and leaned back. We were both quiet as we watched the sky change colors for several moments. It was full with an explosion of magnificent colors that soon faded to yet another color and looked like bunches of ribbons flung across the heavens. God was an incredible artist with an inconceivable palette.

"Tea?" she said as she began to pour from a flowered teapot into a matching teacup. The antique set was beautiful. As I put two lumps of sugar into my cup, she disappeared into the house and came back with two bowls of peach cobbler with a dash of cinnamon and a splash of heavy cream.

"Your mother used to have tea with me from this very tea set," she commented. My head jerked up. Talk about surprised!

"My…mother?" I choked out.

"Yes, your mother. Kathleen worked for me at the general store and would come here after we closed just to relax a little and talk about the day. She was a hard worker, learned fast. She had a head for business, and I was interested in opening a store in another small town, and I wanted her to run it. But her husband didn't like that idea, so I let her run the Fiddyment store while I opened up the new one and got it going." She stopped and allowed me to absorb that news.

"Lucy, do you remember much about your mother?" she continued.

It took me a moment to savor and swallow a mouthful of the peach cobbler before I could answer. Words tumbled out of my mouth.

"Not a whole lot. I was four when she died. I have her picture so I know what she looked like, and every so often I'll get a whiff of a fragrance that I think she used to wear, but I don't know what it was. And, of course, I know what people have told me about her through the years. How she liked to sing, and wade in the creek, and play badminton, and that she was learning to quilt, and she adored children. I think I remember stretching out with her on the grass and watching clouds form into shapes, and we made snow angels in the winter." I stopped to reach back into my brain for more memories of my mother.

"And I remember her being in bed a lot, and she let me brush her hair...and people brought food over...and there was one woman in particular who helped care for her." My eyes squinted as I thought about that memory. "My dad didn't seem to like her, and I remember that he said mean things to her and that she was entirely too difficult to please, and he called her a witch and told her to get out! Later he told me that that 'witch woman' wouldn't be coming back and I should stop crying." And he said, "She is just too persnickety for her own good and we don't need her." Wow. I wondered where that memory came from.

Pearl reached over and touched my hand, and it was then I knew. Pearl *was* that woman. And it was my very own father who inadvertently named her persnickety witch.

"Actually, my dear," Pearl began, "my married name is Witsche, spelled slightly different than what you might think. Your father wasn't calling me witch at all. But a four-year-old little girl didn't understand that, and she referred to me as the persnickety witch every time she saw me. Oh, the way you used to say persnickety, it never did come out right. The older people in town knew the play on words, and they thought the little girl was very clever. And, after all, I *am* persnickety and stuck in my ways, and I like things done right."

"It was *me*?" I asked incredulously. "I'm the one who started all that? Oh, Pearl…I am so sorry."

And then the humor hit me, and I laughed so hard I thought my sides would split. We both laughed loud and long, and both of us had tears spilling down our cheeks. Chester stretched, stood, rubbed against our legs, and meowed to let us know his concern.

"Oh my goodness," I said between snorts and giggles. "Instead of 'persnickety witch,' you are Pearl Witsche."

"One and the same," she said with a huge grin after sipping the hot tea.

"Oh my, I just don't remember that part. The next that I do remember is that my dad left and his sister, Auntie Caroline, came to stay with me…moved right into our house…and she tried—oh, how she tried—to become my mother, and I resisted like crazy."

"You stayed with me until Caroline arrived…slept in Michael's room. You loved the circus that he whittled," Pearl told me.

"I did? I mean, I stayed with you? Gosh, I just don't remember that," I said.

"I let you have the circus animals and after Caroline arrived and settled in, she wouldn't let you keep them. She came into the general store and threw them on the counter. I came over to your house one day when you were at school and told Caroline that Kathleen had some of my things and I wanted them back. She let me in and I took your baby book, photo albums, your booties, many of your baby toys and clothes, the quilt she had started, a dulcimer I'd given her, many of Mike's whittlings, and I have everything in a trunk inside the house. I didn't know if she would keep those precious things or not, and I was determined to get as much as I could and keep them for you."

"You have my things? Pictures? Things that my mother made? And Michael's circus?" I asked. "Penelope told me that somebody bought Michael's circus…"

"Yes, somebody did." Her eyes sparkled and got as big as saucers. "Me! He asked me if he could sell some of his whittles in the store, and I adored what he had done with the circus, so I bought it," she told me.

"Hmmm…there's a chill in the air. Why don't we go inside?" Pearl asked as she got up. "Do you like the cobbler?"

"Yes, it's absolutely wonderful," I answered.

"It's your mother's recipe. She was quite the cook and baker. She could bake almost anything. I think I even rescued some of her recipes!"

The screen door lightly closed behind us, and I entered Pearl's living room.

Chapter 3

Pearl's living room wasn't at all what I expected. Instead, I found it tastefully decorated with overstuffed furniture upholstered in cabbage rose chintz, a cranberry-colored velvet chaise in the corner, a rocking chair with a comfy cushion, an upright piano and bench, some framed pictures on top of the piano, her hammered dulcimer was on a stand, and there was beautiful artwork, tatted doilies, and lots of oak pieces. She gave me time to wander around and examine things and answer my questions. I touched several ebony and ivory keys of the piano. It was out of tune. Then I picked up a photograph of a man in a uniform and asked, "Is this Michael?" and she nodded that it was. When I got to the fireplace, I noticed the fine carving of the mantelpiece, vases of freshly cut flowers, and little wooden figures placed here and there.

"This owl," Pearl said, "is the very first piece that Michael ever whittled...it's a whistle," and she put it to her lips and blew. It sounded like a train whistle off in the distance. "And this man is his father. See how his legs hang over the mantel? Here's the tent to the circus collection. He used to tell me that he could look at a piece of wood and roll it over in his hands until it told him what he should whittle. See this piece here? I was always amazed at how he could get the pipe in the fella's mouth and the grin just right and the twinkle in his eye."

A portrait of Pearl and Willowby when they were younger had a place of honor over the fireplace. They were quite a handsome couple. Michael had hand-carved the frame. and it was remarkable and perfect.

"It was painted from a picture taken on our wedding day at my parents' estate in Virginia. We had a beautiful outdoor wedding in the garden and a cake, and champagne reception in the atrium and dancing in the ballroom."

Pearl's face glowed as she remembered the day and told me about some of the prominent guests who had attended.

"Let's go open that trunk and see your things," Pearl suggested.

She took me through the dining room where I noticed Michael's carving of "The Last Supper," and I made a mental note to look at it closely later, and then we entered her bedroom. I quickly glanced around. It was large, spacious, had oak hardwood floors covered by braided area rugs; it was feminine and dainty, the headboard had Pearl's initials, *P.O.W.*, carved into it; a gorgeous antique dresser stood against one wall. An oak dressing vanity with a half-circle mirror was angled in one corner and it had a round stool. An exquisite oak camelback trunk stood at the foot of the bed and it was covered with a lacey throw. Pearl handed me a pillow and said, "Here, sit on this," and I dropped it to the floor and did as I was told. She pulled the vanity's stool over close to the trunk and opened the lid before she sat. The lace throw slid to the floor, and I could see the leather handles, tin panels, and cast-iron bolts and latches. The chest was stuffed full with trinkets and treasures.

"Everything in here belongs to you," Pearl said as she picked up a pink crocheted blanket and held it close to her face. A familiar fragrance arose from the trunk.

"Pearl," I began, "I think I can smell my mother's fragrance. Is it here?"

"I don't remember," Pearl said, "but if it is, it will be closer to the bottom."

Pearl handed the blanket to me, and I moved my hands over its softness and examined the white satin border. It was lovely. Next there were my white christening dress, bonnet, and tiny white shoes. Various other baby outfits had been lovingly wrapped in tissue paper and were stacked with an occasional rattle or baby toy tucked in between. Pearl and I *ooh*ed and *aah*ed over each item. They had kept their colors nicely after being tucked away for all these years.

Underneath the clothing, blankets, and soft items were books, squares to a wedding ring quilt, photo albums, a wooden plaque with the words *Lucille, Bringer of Light*, darling stuffed animals, toys, Raggedy Ann and Andy, a book of Mother's handwritten recipes, and Michael's whittles. One book in particular captured my attention. It was *The First Year of Lucille Olivia Baldwin,* and my mother had written in it almost every day. It had a page delegated for guests and their gifts, another for "firsts"—first word, first step, first birthday, and potty training firsts—a page with an envelope for a locket of hair (mine was blond and very wavy), a page for likes and dislikes, and a page for favorites. It also listed weights and measures. Every now and then I would say, "Oh, Pearl, look what she wrote here…" and she would say something appropriate, such as, "Oh my, how sweet" or "Oh yes! I remember that!"

I couldn't wait to delve into the photo albums and other miscellaneous things toward the bottom, but it was getting late and Pearl suggested that I take a few of the things home to show Tom and the children, and bring Tom over at another time to actually take the trunk. It was heavy enough empty!

As I stood to gather my things and embrace this wonderful persnickety witch, I realized that I was emotionally spent. Pearl had bent over and was carefully looking for something in the trunk. At last she stood with a smile on her face, and she handed me a bottle of Chanel No. 5. Around it was a little gold chain, and hanging from the chain was a baby's ring.

"The fragrance! She wore Chanel," I whispered excitedly. "But what's this?" and I touched the tiny ring.

"That's your baby ring, my dear. I gave it to you the day you were christened." Pearl told me that she didn't want to lose anything that day years ago when she gathered my possessions, and that was the only way she could think of to remove the bottle of perfume and the baby jewelry so that the chain didn't get all tangled.

We walked out onto the porch together and carefully navigated the stairs. My head and arms were loaded with things from my past, and we carefully placed the treasures in the backseat of the T-Bird. I got in, waved good-bye, and drove down the gravel driveway. It was a clear night, with a star-studded sky and a crescent moon peeking from just behind the weeping willow tree. Two shooting stars traveled through the night sky, one chasing the other. They reminded me of Pearl and me and our chance meeting.

As Pearl was getting ready for bed, the telephone rang.

"Aunt Pearl? How are you doing?" said a deep bass voice.

"Michael. It's so nice to hear from you. How are things in Chicago?" Pearl asked. He brought her up-to-date on family things and his newest work project. His twin children, a boy and girl—who looked nothing alike; the son looked like his mother, the daughter looked like her father—had just turned sixteen. They were named after their parents, so the girl was named Abigail Olivia after Gail, and she shared Pearl's middle name, and the boy was Michael Gabriel. The twins had decided when they were five and entering kindergarten that they wanted to be called Abby and Gabby and had stood before Michael and Gail to give their mom and dad instructions.

"We want you to call us Abby and Gabby, not Abigail and Michael, because we want to have rhyming names," Abby said before Gabby interrupted.

"And we don't want you to dress us alike or even put us in the same color or anything like that. That would be *yucky*!" he said as he wrinkled his nose, putting much emphasis on yucky. Then the four of them shook hands on it to make it official.

Michael and Gail somehow managed to keep straight faces and stifle their giggles until the twins marched out of the room, then there were gales of laughter. Brothers and sisters are often very close, but the twins knew what the other was thinking, and they were there for each other emotionally, physically, and spiritually. Growing up all too fast, they were now juniors in high school, and very anxious to get their driver's licenses.

"Aunt Pearl! Aunt Pearl!" Abby was giggling and yelling toward the phone. Finally, Michael handed it to her. "We want to thank you for the gold bars. What a cool present!" Then Gabby yelled with her, "Thank you!" And they were gone.

Pearl laughed and knew she wouldn't be able to get a word in edgewise when Abby and Gabby were around, but finally she said, "You're so very welcome, kiddles."

She paused for just a moment then said, “I have so much to tell you, Michael. I kept bumping into Lucy last week—first in her yard, then outside the general store, and finally at Pearl’s Gate, so I knew she was curious about the persnickety witch. We chatted a little, and I invited her to come over this evening. We opened the trunk.”

“Oh, wow. You did? How did that go?” he asked.

“I think very well. She now knows that I’m not a witch, and she learned some things about her mother,” Pearl said. “We laughed about the ‘witch confusion’ until our sides hurt!”

Chapter 4

"Honey, I'm home..." I said as I went in the back door into the kitchen. Tom was sitting at the kitchen table doing a crossword puzzle. He looked up and smiled at me. "And guess what I've got to tell you?"

"So, is the old girl as bad as you thought?" Tom asked.

"Heavens, no! She's incredible. Wonderful. Charming. And certainly not a witch. But, did you know that her last name is Witsche?" I could barely get the words out fast enough.

"Wait a minute, slow down," Tom said.

"Well, there are some things in the backseat. If you help me bring them in, I can start to show you," and I pulled him to his feet. "I wish you could've been there with me, Tom. I know! Let's have her over for a meal. That way the children can get to know her too. I know Cathy would enjoy being around her. How about Sunday?"

Tom stopped beside the car and stood with his arms stretched out so I could load him up.

"How'd she get these things?" he asked.

"It's a long story. Just wait 'til you hear it," I answered as I yawned. "I'm so glad tomorrow is Saturday."

"I wonder if she still has that old car," Tom said more to himself than me. "She showed it to me once when I was dropping off some groceries. It was something else. Huge. Gorgeous. I'd love to drive it."

Once inside their bedroom, Tom carefully put his armload of things onto the seat of a chair and picked up the bottle of Chanel. He raised his eyebrows and looked toward me.

"That was my mom's fragrance," I explained. "Pearl gave me the baby ring on the day I was christened."

"Really? Interesting..." he said. He removed the chain from the bottle so he could examine the ring closely. "I wonder if...yes, look right here...she had it engraved. Man! Is that ever tiny! But it says..."

I came closer so I could see. "It says 'POW to LOB, 1940.' from Pearl to me. Isn't this just so, so...special?" I groped for just the right word.

I sat on the side of the bed, thinking about the things Pearl had told me. Tom sat beside me and said, "Honey, let's look at everything tomorrow when you're fresh. Okay?"

I nodded and said, "Yeah, you're right. The bed is going to feel awfully good. Would you put the Chanel on the dresser...and the chain and ring? I want to know exactly where they are in the morning."

Tom had gone into the bathroom, so I removed the bed covering and lay down. My head sank into the comfort of the pillow and I guess I drifted off because the next morning, my shoes were off, but I was still wearing the sundress. I stretched, yawned, and wondered what day it was. *Oh yeah, Saturday. Thank goodness!* I could hear Tom downstairs singing very off-key with Nat King Cole on the radio. I smelled coffee and bacon. I yelled downstairs, "Hey, honey! Do I have time for a shower?" He danced over to the bottom of the stairs with Cathy riding the tops of his feet, holding on for dear life.

"Yeah, sure. I'll start the pancakes in five minutes. how's that?" he said as he and Cathy twirled through the hallway back toward the kitchen.

After my shower, I stood in front of a mirror and noticed that there was a chain around my neck.

"Hmmm? What's this?" I wondered out loud. I looked closer and saw the tiny ring. *I got myself a honey of a hubby,* I thought.

I loved the mornings that Tom cooked. He went all out and even had warmed the syrup. A huge stack of pancakes sat in the middle of the round table, and all the accompaniments along the outside. I immediately went over to him, hugged and kissed him, and whispered something in his ear that made him turn bright red. Cathy got embarrassed and giggled. Jameson stuffed more pancake into his mouth. I just knew he was going to be a sticky mess, so I kissed his forehead and patted his tummy when I went past him.

"Good morning, Little Man," I said to him. "You're certainly enjoying that pancake."

"Hey, Cathy with a C, look what Pearl gave me on the day I was baptized. I bent over beside her and gently pulled the ring up so she could see it.

"Oh, Mama, it's so little…and beautiful," Cathy whispered.

"What else did you get?"

"Well, the best thing is that I got memories. Memories of my own mother. Your grandmother. And photo albums and some things that I brought home that I'll show you later. Okay? Let's eat. I'm starving. Pass the stack, Mack."

After breakfast, Cathy and I were dusting the things in the living room and she asked, "Mama, are we going to do something fun with Daddy today?"

"I haven't talked to Daddy yet, but I thought we might go on a picnic and play in Fiddyment Creek at the little sandy shoreline," I answered.

We hadn't heard Tom come into the house from mowing the lawn, but he leaned against the doorway and said, "Sure. With one condition. Only if we can take the inner tubes and float downstream a little. And make a sandcastle, right, Buddy?" Tom directed that question toward Jameson.

We hurried to finish the house chores so we could go. Tom got the kids ready while I put things into the picnic basket and grabbed some things we'd probably need, including a plastic bucket and shovel for Jameson. Cathy sang "Row, Row, Row Your Boat," and it didn't take long for all of us to join into the rotation and sing at the top of our lungs. I think we must've been quite a sight driving down the tree-lined street, around the square, through town, and ending up where locals would go to swim and play on a hot summer day. A few years back, somebody had made a sign that said *Put Shoes Here.* And so we did.

"Hey! There's Mr. Maguire's car!" we heard a voice yell. Then four of Tom's high school students appeared, kicked their shoes and flip-flops off at the sign, grabbed Jameson and Cathy, and ran into the creek and played, splashed, teased, and laughed. Our kids remembered this bunch from last summer when one of the girls had given Jameson swimming lessons. He was like a little fish and kicked and dog paddled from student to student. I was all settled on a blanket with my book, but I kept thinking about Pearl, my mother, and the things we had talked about the night before. So I put the book away and watched the kids frolic in the water. Tom came out of the water and sat in the sand and piled sand into the bucket. Jameson waddled out of the water and sat down with a squishy sound.

"Hey, c'mon, let's go to the rope swing," one of the teens suggested. "Can we take Cathy and Jameson?"

"No, not today," I answered. "You guys go on and have fun. I think we'll have lunch while you're gone. I've got extra cookies for you when you come back."

Tom and Jameson finished the castle, and he brought the kids up to the blanket where I had spread out the food, which they heartily gobbled up. We all were very relaxed and having fun. I listened to the kids chatter and smiled. I felt very content with my life and even with the newest piece of information I had just received last night from Pearl. I had so many questions for her and I wanted to know more about my mother.

The creek was maybe four feet deep and crystal clear. It was a perfect summer day. Jameson was riding with me on an inner tube, and I pointed out things along the way. Tom and Cathy were floating behind us and they were skipping stones.

At one point she yelled to me, "I can't imagine this creek as a mean old river that killed Mr. Witsche and that other man."

"Neither can I, Cathy," I hollered back.

We could see the sandy bottom, rocks, some fish, plants that grow in the water, and a turtle. I explained to Jameson that the rocks were smooth from years and years of being exposed to the water. Jameson was on his tummy hanging over the side of the inner tube, and his feet were dangling in the center. I let my fingers drift in the water as we floated along the banks of Fiddyment Creek. Eventually, we could tell that we were getting close to the rope swing because we could hear the kids making the noise of Tarzan. As we got closer, I yelled to watch out for hippopotami. They hooted and hollered and waved to us as we floated by.

In the car on the way home, the children dozed in the backseat and I said, "Honey, we haven't talked about this yet, but what do you think about having Pearl over tomorrow? We could grill burgers and chicken and keep the mess outside, and the kids can play in the yard. I don't even think I need to go to the store."

"Yeah, sure. It sounds fun. I'm curious about Persnick too," he said. "Let's call her when we get home."

"Do you think she knows how to play croquet?" Cathy asked. She had stirred and heard just enough, then fell asleep again.

After the dishes were in the dishwasher, I picked up the phone and dialed Pearl's number.

"Oh, my goodness," Pearl said. "I was on the other side of the house. How are you, dear?"

"We're all great, Pearl. Tom and I were wondering if you'd join us for an early supper tomorrow afternoon? You will? Lovely! Tom will come and pick you up around four o'clock."

There. That was done. After the kids were in bed, Tom and I looked at the photo albums and other things I brought home, and I told him about my visit with Pearl.

"Do you know why your dad left in such a hurry?" Tom asked.

"No, I don't," I answered, "but I bet Pearl does."

Chapter 5

The dust billowed around the car as Tom drove up the gravel driveway. Pearl was waiting on the porch, and she let him get out of the car and practically race up her porch stairs. He grabbed her shoulders and gave her a big bear hug.

"Hey, Persnick! How ya doing?" Tom said.

"Oh, Thomas, you handsome man, you haven't changed at all since you were here…how long ago?" Pearl said. She was holding a basket of vegetables from her garden and Tom took it from her.

"Do you think Lucy would like these?" she asked.

"Sure as shootin'," he replied. "We especially love tomatoes. Mmmmmm, good. But what's this?" He held up an interesting small, round vegetable.

"Kohlrabi," said Pearl.

"Kohl-whaty?" he asked.

"Kohlrabi. It's in the cabbage family," she told him. "Just try it."

"You bet. We'll have just a *little* coleslaw tonight made from your whatzit," he said as he winked at her.

She took him into the house to get the trunk, and he skillfully got it out to the car and into the backseat. As the shiny T-Bird rumbled down the driveway, he asked her if he should put the top up.

"Heavens, no!" she exclaimed. "The breeze is wonderful. This car is almost as big as mine," she commented.

"You still have it?" he asked.

"The Bentley? I most certainly do, but I haven't driven it in a very long time. I don't even know if it starts," she said.

"If you want, I can check it out for you," Tom said.

The Maguire household was filled with excited anticipation, and I had a hard time getting the kids to settle down.

"They're here," I said to Cathy and Jameson. "Just behave yourselves."

Pearl came through the screen door and paused for a moment before she walked into my open arms.

Pearl had a tear in her eye as she said, "It's different, but the same. I love what you've done to make it your own. You know, I haven't been in here since the day I gathered your things."

"Would you like to see the rest of it?" I asked her.

After a quick tour of the big old Victorian home that had been left to me in my mother's will, we went to the back porch where I had lemonade waiting. The porch was screened, and it had cooled off a little from the early afternoon heat. Plus, the ceiling fan was lazily going around and around, moving the air.

"Pearl," I began, "I'm wearing the chain and baby ring, and I noticed an inscription with our initials," and I pulled it away from my neck to show her. "Here's my first question, and I probably have hundreds: Your initials are P-O-W and mine were L-O-B, now L-O-M. What does *your o* stand for?"

"Olivia," she said smiling, "as does yours. Your mother and I were very good friends, and that's the way she named you after me. She thought that Pearl would be too old-fashioned and that Olivia was very elegant."

Cathy was seated beside me on the porch swing and piped up, "What about your husband? What were his initials?"

"Well, Miss Cathy with a C, his name was Willowby Oliver Witsche, so W-O-W. They are at the top of the general store. They're fading, but they're there. And the fact that our middle initials were both *o* was purely coincidental."

"His initials spell *wow*, you know," Cathy said with much certainty.

"Yes, they do," Pearl said, "and mine spell *pow*!" Pearl made a fist and held it up.

"Pearl, how long was my mother sick?" I asked.

"I think you were a newborn when she found the lump. She let it go and didn't mention it to anyone, not even me. I'm not sure when she finally went to the doctor, but the cancer had already spread into the lymph nodes. She worked for me at the general store on her good days. She had a wonderful older lady that came here to the house to take care of you. And on some weekends, your daddy was here," Pearl explained.

Tom came up to the porch and took a sweating glass of lemonade. He held the glass to his face to cool off a little before taking a big gulp.

"Persnick—" he began.

"Tom! Don't call her that," I said chiding him.

"Honey, I've always called her Persnick—right, Persnick?" he said. "I didn't know you had anything to do with that name until last night. Anyway…Persnick, what was Lucy's dad like? Was he a good guy? What did he do? Why didn't he stick around after Kathleen died?"

"Well, let me put it this way. At that time, he was a car salesman. He liked the brew and he liked the ladies. When Kathleen passed on and he learned that she had left everything to Lucy in the will, he saw it as an easy out to get his sister here so he could skedaddle. And he definitely didn't like me being here and made that perfectly clear. When Caroline came, she promised him that she wouldn't let me around Lucy and she kept her word. *Hmph!* What's she up to these days?" Pearl asked.

"Ohhhhhh, she died a couple of years ago," Lucy said.

"Well, I'm sorry about that. The good thing is that she was willing to come take care of you, and in all fairness, she did a fine job raising you," Pearl said.

"Pearl, how did you and my mother meet?" I asked.

"It was a hot summer evening at a church ice cream social held on the square. We were supposed to sit beside someone we didn't know and tell them a lie and also tell them a truth. Later, they were supposed to tell each statement and which one they thought was the truth. I sat beside her at the fountain and we took turns. She said, 'I'm pregnant. I hate roller coasters,' and I said, 'I'm a witch. I was on the Titanic.' She didn't know which to believe and when it was her turn, she explained her dilemma. The little crowd didn't know what to think either, and they finally asked me which one was true. I told them, 'They both are true. My last name is Witsche, and I had been on the Titanic before she launched and made her fateful maiden voyage.' So, you see, it's how you say things that might cause confusion or clarity. Kathleen and I stayed long after the ice cream social was over, and we talked and talked, and we were very comfortable with each other. Before long, the bell tower struck midnight, and we scurried away like Cinderella's mice."

"Hold that thought," Tom said. "Let's eat. May I assist you, Madame?" Tom said as he stood before Pearl and escorted her to the table overlooking the garden.

"Mama, Mama," Cathy loudly whispered to me, "what am I supposed to call her?"

Pearl turned and bent over to Cathy's ear and whispered, "Why don't you call me Aunt Pearl? I would like that, Cathy with a C."

"Lucy, how is your lilac bush doing?" Pearl asked as she spread the napkin on her lap.

I just looked at her while another memory emerged from my brain. I remembered my mother and Pearl planting the lilac bush as well as many others plants that had grown into gorgeous specimens and now enhanced my yard. They would get down on all fours and dig and giggle, plant, and water.

"Ah. This past spring, the lilac bushes were full with blossoms, and the fragrance was phenomenal. It's a pity the lilacs don't last longer. I think I had them in every room of the house! And the peonies were very showy also. Had you and my mother finished planting everything you wanted?" I asked.

"I don't remember, dear," Pearl said. "Let's take a look after dinner."

Cathy had been taught that when people were finished eating, they were to put their forks with tines down off the right edge of the plate, and she watched with an eagle eye so she could tell if Pearl knew that too. As Pearl placed her fork in the "finished" position, Cathy looked at me and I nodded "yes." She had helped me make the dessert and couldn't wait to show it off. We cleared the table and Cathy said to Pearl in a very adult tone when she passed by her, "I think you'll enjoy dessert, Aunt Pearl. It's called flower sundae."

Jameson looked at me with a quizzical expression. He loved to eat flower sundaes.

She came out of the kitchen carrying a tray with five plastic flowerpots, each with a single stem flower. She placed one in front of Pearl and Pearl's face lit up, her eyes got big, and she said to Cathy, "This looks delightful! Tell me, please, how you make flower sundaes."

"Well," said Cathy, "first you make brownies, then you break them into pieces in a bowl. If you make chocolate brownies, then it looks like dirt in the flowerpot. Then you add ice cream that's melted a little. Then you stir it up. Then you put some into the plastic flowerpots. Then you cut a straw in half. Then you put half a straw into the center. Then you put them in the freezer. When you're ready, you take them out and put a flower into the straw! See? It's easy!"

"Oh, my goodness! Did you think that up?" Pearl asked.

"Naw, it's my mama's recipe," Cathy said proudly. "We make fun stuff all the time."

After dinner, Tom put the kids to bed while Pearl and I strolled arm in arm through the yard and garden. She stopped to admire many of the flowers then she said, "You know, your mother and I made a map of the yard and where we were going to plant certain flowers or bushes and everything seems to be here. But I don't remember doing all this. Do you think your Aunt Caroline found the map and finished it?"

"I remember that she spent lots of time out here watering and weeding, but I don't remember if she planted. Perhaps," I said.

"Well, no matter. It's beautiful, and I hope you're enjoying it. You're doing a fine job of taking care of it. You must have Kathleen's green thumb."

In the living room, Pearl and I sat side by side, looking at one of the photo albums and chattering away. Tom joined us and sat in the recliner across the room.

"Pearl," I said, "where did my mother's money come from? I never seemed to want for anything. Why didn't she leave anything to my father? Was it passed down from her parents? What happened to them? Would you know any of that?"

"Good questions, hon," Tom said.

"Well, you *are* full of questions. And rightly so. Some of it I can help you understand. I don't think we'll talk about all of it tonight. There's far too much to tell. During her pregnancy with you and as we became such good friends, she told me about her relationship with your father (which wasn't very good), and that the house had been a gift to her by your grandparents. I suggested that she take out a life insurance policy listing you as the beneficiary. Now keep in mind at that point, we had no idea that she would find a lump a few months later. And I also suggested that she meet with my attorney and write a will which stated her explicit desires. As the months passed and she got sicker and sicker and we knew she was going to die, I told your parents that I would be more than happy to adopt you. By then I had seen your father's true colors, but he wouldn't hear of it. You would 'stay with the Baldwin family,' said he. And that's how Caroline moved in. On my own, I started a trust for Kathleen and her heirs and when she died, the life insurance money went into the Powwow Trust, which I administered."

"Powwow? You mean like a meeting of Indians?" I asked.

"No, no, no," Pearl said. "Look at the letters. They're my and Willow's initials. But I'm happy to see that it did just as I hoped. When you got monthly checks while you were away at college, they were from Powwow Trust."

"Really. Oh my gosh! You're absolutely right. But, of course, I never made the connection."

"Everything was to go to you in stages, but into the trust so that I could guard it. After Kathleen died, your father wanted to leave. He really had nothing, not even a place to live because of the will's wording. That's when you stayed with me until Caroline arrived, which was just a little more than two weeks. But my, how I loved having you. It was then that I began to invest in stock for you. Also, I have twenty-five bars of gold in a safe place for you. At today's prices, that is a lot of money. And even though I honored your father's wishes and didn't get involved in your life, I managed to get involved in those financial ways until you were ready to have me in your life again. Does that clear things up?"

"Yes, of course. Ummm, exactly how much money are we talking about? Hundreds? Thousands?" I asked.

"Heavens, yes! We'll have to go to the Powwow Office and see. I just made some more investments which are doing very well," Pearl answered. "And now, I should be going home. This has been a perfectly lovely evening. Thank you so much. Thomas? Will you do the honors?"

"Yes, of course. Lucy, I'll be back in a little bit. Wait up for me? Wow, Persnick, what an evening we've had," he said as he and Pearl left the house.

In the car, they were both quiet. Finally, he said, "Persnick, years ago, you put a little bug in my ear that Lucy would be a good catch. That's when I started noticing her, watching her, seeing what she was all about, and dating her. I fell in love with Lucy, the person. I had no idea she was rich! Do you think she'll change now that she knows she has all this money? Persnick?" he said as he glanced at her.

Pearl stared at him with a wild, a confused look in her eyes, and she didn't seem to comprehend what Tom was saying. When she tried to speak, it sounded like gobbledygook. One side of her mouth drooped.

"Pearl? Are you feeling okay?"

She didn't answer.

"Okay, young lady, we're going to the hospital."

He did a U-turn and drove as fast as he could toward the hospital in the neighboring town. At the emergency room driveway, he laid on the horn and people in hospital uniforms came rushing out. They put Pearl on a gurney and Tom stopped at the desk to give them what information he knew. Then he went to the pay phone to call Lucy.

"Sit down, honey," he said. "I don't know exactly what's going on, but Pearl started to act confused and she had difficulty communicating with me, so I took her to the hospital. I think I may know where she keeps phone numbers at her house, so I'm going to go look and contact Michael, then I'll come home. I figured you would want to come to the hospital."

"Yes, I do. Thank you," I said. "Be sure to tell Michael that we're praying for Pearl and for them."

Tom climbed Pearl's porch stairs two at a time and went into the house. He saw a little desk with a phone on it and opened a drawer. Yes! There was an address/phone book.

"Morgan, Morgan, Morgan," he said as his eyes skimmed down the page.

"Michael? This is Tom Maguire. Your aunt spent the evening with us and when I was taking her home, she wasn't acting quite right. So I took her to Mercy Hospital. No, I don't know what the diagnosis is. The doctors in the emergency room were doing an EKG, hooking her up to oxygen, starting to do some tests. The business office isn't open at this hour, but do you know where she might keep her medical insurance papers? When I get home, Lucy will head over to be with her." He paused for a minute, then said, "Sure. Whatever we can do to help."

I spent the night in Pearl's room and I was dozing in the chair beside Pearl's bed when Michael and Gail came in. They stood beside the bed, whispering, and I finally realized that they weren't the nursing staff.

I stood to my feet and said, "Michael. After all these years, I'm so happy to finally meet you, but not like this. And Gail." I hugged both of them. "Where are the kiddles?" I asked.

"We left them home...they have summer school today," Gail answered. "But we're close enough. We'll make sure that they get over here soon. They do love their Aunt Pearl."

"Lucy, have you talked to the doctors? Do you know what happened?" Michael asked.

"No, the nursing staff told me that she was resting comfortably and they let me stay here all night, that's about all I know," I said. "They came in several times through the night."

"Do you know if Tom found the insurance papers?" Michael asked.

"I don't think so," I said.

"They are probably at the Powwow Office. I'll go get them in a bit. Is she coherent?" Michael asked me.

"Yes, but there's some mild paralysis on her left side. And her speech is a little slurred," I said.

We heard a grunt. Pearl had awakened. "H'lo," she said with a raspy voice that didn't sound like hers. There were some other sounds, and we all decided she was happy to see Michael and Gail. Michael leaned over, kissed her cheek, squeezed her hand, and asked her where she kept the medical insurance papers—at home? No. At the Powwow Office? Yes.

Michael left and I said to Gail, "You know, Gail, Pearl, and I just reconnected after all these years, and she has told me about many of the pieces to the puzzle of my life. You never know how everything is going to fit together. But I'm so glad to have the mystery of the persnickety witch solved. Can you believe that I caused all that grief?"

"She waited for you for a long time, Lucy. I, for one, am very glad that part is over," Gail said. "But it surely was funny!"

Pearl stuck up one thumb as her means of agreement.

While Pearl took an afternoon nap and had more testing, Michael and Gail came over to our house for lunch and some rest. He found the papers and contacted her personal physician. Jameson and Cathy were polite and not quite sure how to act since they had just spent the evening with Pearl, and now she was hospitalized. Gail and I assured Cathy that we thought Pearl would be fine, but it might take some time for her to complete physical therapy.

Cathy had something on her mind and couldn't wait to share it. "Mama," she said, "could Aunt Pearl come stay with us when she gets out of the hospital? I could read to her and get things for her. Whatever she needed! Please, Mama, please?"

"Cathy, I think that's a grand idea. But we'll need to talk to all parties concerned, okay?" I looked at Gail and she shrugged her shoulders and kind of nodded her head in agreement.

Tom just smiled his approval and said, "We've already got the downstairs guest room waiting for a guest. It wouldn't take much at all to get it ready for Pearl."

"Well," I said, "the only votes we need are from Pearl and Michael."

"All right, you guys, exactly what am I voting on?" Michael asked as he came in through the back door.

"If Pearl could stay here for her period of recuperation. I'm not working. The kids love her. Tom has the marching band rehearsals each afternoon until school starts, but for now that's it. I could help her, take her to the doctor or wherever she needed to go," I said.

"I take it the rest of you have voted in the affirmative?" he asked as he looked around the room. "Then it's okay with me. I'd certainly rest easier. The old gal might need a little bit of persuasion though."

Later in the afternoon, Michael and Gail left for the hospital for a visit, then stopped by our house to tell us their plans before returning to Chicago. Michael told us that Pearl was willing to come stay with us, the doctor had come in, verified that she'd had a stroke, and said he wanted to keep her there for about a week. She kept saying something they couldn't understand.

"It sounded like '*che chedder,*'" he said. "Che chedder... what on earth could that be?"

I think all of us scratched our heads trying to figure it out.

I usually get up around two thirty to peek in on the kids. We'd recently taken the side rails off Jameson's bed so he could have a "big boy bed," but he slept restlessly. Tonight he was on his tummy with one leg hanging over the edge. I was repositioning him in the bed when it came to me. *Well I'll be. Che chedder... Check Chester!* I thought to myself. She's worried about the cat.

Chapter 6

I was in the guest room looking to see what needed to be done so that Pearl would be comfortable while she stayed with us when I heard my doorbell ringing over and over. I could see through the oval beveled window of the large wooden door that it was Penelope and she looked absolutely frantic. Paulie stood in front of her and peered through the glass.

"Hi there, neighbor," I said as I swung the door open wide. "Come on in. Let's have a cup of coffee. I've got lots to tell you. Paulie, want to play with Jameson? He and Cathy are out back. Go through the kitchen, okay?"

Penelope sat at my kitchen table and said, "I've been so worried about you and the witch! I haven't seen you since last Friday! And she hasn't ridden past on her bike for the last two mornings. I certainly hope she's all right."

"First, Penelope, let me tell you that we're fine, and Pearl will be fine. Sorry, I don't have muffins or anything like that to offer you. Life has been, well, rather hectic. I don't even know where to begin."

Because I was still processing so much information (and because it was nobody's business), I told her the basics and left out all the details about my inheritance, Powwow Trust, and my current financial condition. Penelope thought it extremely funny that I had been the one to innocently start the rumors of the persnickety witch, and she admired the chain and baby ring around my neck.

"So now we're getting the guest room ready for Pearl. She'll be staying here to recuperate," I said.

"Mama, Mama, come quick!" It was Cathy. "Paulie fell in the rose bushes and his nose is bleeding!"

We rushed outside to see this latest catastrophe and discovered that he had examined a bug on the rose stem a little too closely and a thorn pierced his skin. I cleaned him off and he was good as new.

"Well, I'm glad to hear that everything is okay," said Penelope as she corralled Paulie to take him home. "I guess we won't be seeing Pearl on her bike for a while."

"Thanks for your concern for all of us, Penelope," I said and I meant it. "When she's up to it, we'll have you over for coffee or hot tea and you can get to know the wonderful 'witch woman' too," I said as I closed the front door.

My life had always been an open book. I decided it wasn't, at least for now.

"Hey, kids! Let's go over to Pearl's house and check on things!" I yelled.

We piled into the car and drove the short distance to Pearl's cottage. As we climbed the stairs to the porch, I held an empty suitcase in one hand and Jameson's hand in the other; I asked Cathy to stick close by. "Don't touch *anything* unless I tell you to," I cautioned them.

We went into Pearl's bedroom and found some things she would need at the hospital and at our house. I also found a book she'd been reading, and her Bible on the nightstand. Her address/phone book was on the telephone table where Tom had left it.

"Cathy, go to the kitchen and see if you can spot her straw hat and bring it here," I said.

"Mama, there's a big black cat in here!" Cathy yelled. "And I found her straw hat!"

I put the now-packed suitcase by the front door and went to the kitchen. Cathy was squatting down stroking Chester's head and back; he was loving the attention, and purring like crazy.

"Oh, good. I'm glad you found him. This is Chester. I think he should come home with us so he'll be used to things when Pearl gets there. She'll be happy to see him," I said as I showed Jameson how to pet him.

I loaded everything into the car—including a big basket of vegetables we'd picked in the garden—and the children and cat were in the backseat. Cathy said, "You know what, Mama? Aunt Pearl is more like my gammy than my aunt."

I replied, "Yes, I know what you mean."

Back at our house, Becky dropped over to return the cookie container and offered to stay with the kids so Tom and I could go to the hospital. Pearl was sitting up in bed, flipping through a magazine. I pulled her hairbrush out of the satchel and asked if she would like me to brush her hair. Her face lit up. I took that as a yes.

"Would you like it up off your neck, Pearl? I have hairpins," I said. She shook her head no.

Tom started asking her a list of questions and waited for her answers as I brushed and she answered the best she could.

"It's your left side that was affected, correct? Are you right-handed? No way. You're a southpaw? Do you need help eating? Have you been up out of bed yet? Have you met with the physical therapist? How about a slate to write on? Would that help? Do you need anything? Who should we contact?"

"Oh!" I said. "Pearl, I went over to your house today and gathered some clothes and toiletries. Here's your Bible and a book, and we brought Chester home with us. Che Chedder. Check Chester. See? I can figure it out. Plus, you'll be back to normal in no time. Is there anything I've forgotten?"

With that she bared her teeth at me.

"You're growling?" I asked, confused.

"No, no, no," Tom said. "She's showing you her teeth. Toothpaste and brush, right, Persnick?"

"Of course. I *did* forget those things. I'm sure the hospital has something for you here, but I'll be sure to get yours, okay?"

She nodded her agreement, then took my hand and started spelling a word in my palm with her right index finger.

"F-R-I-D-A-Y," I said each letter as she marked it.

"Friday. Something's happening on Friday? Is that when you're getting out of here?" I asked.

She smiled.

Throughout that week, we brought the kids over to the hospital for a visit or two; Gail and Michael came with their kids and they spent an entire afternoon at the hospital. We invited them to stay with us for the night.

"Be sure to stop by Pearl's garden and take home anything you can," I told them as they were leaving in the morning. "And have a safe trip home. We'll be sure to let you know how things are going."

Tom and I both had to be at the hospital early to meet with the physical therapist and talk to the doctor before Pearl was released from the hospital. We hung some clothes in the closet, rearranged the furniture; a comfortable chair overlooked the garden, and there was a little side table with a bell that Pearl could ring to call one of us. We had put a vase of flowers on the dresser, a stack of *Ladies Home Journals* and *Reader's Digest*s were on a bedside table, and a little television was there. A slate and chalk were on the bed. Best of all, the room smelled of lavender.

Chapter 7

I think Pearl expected, or at least wanted, to be completely well when she was released from the hospital—and that was not the case. She dragged her left foot when she moved, and her left arm hung limply at her side. She had made huge progress in a very short time, and I kept reminding her of that. The first couple of nights that she was with us, I worried about her and ended up sleeping on the living room sofa in case she needed something in a hurry.

It was now several weeks later on a Monday morning. The kids were just rousing and would be heading downstairs. Pearl was an early riser, so I wasn't worried about her. They just loved having Pearl stay with us and told her so. I think they were good therapy for her.

Jameson knocked on her door and whispered as loud as he could, "Aunt Pearl, you up?"

He timidly cracked open the door and peeked in. Pearl was sitting in the chair, and she smiled and beckoned him in with her right hand. He raced toward her and struggled to climb onto her lap, so she grabbed the back of his pants and pulled him up; he immediately nestled against her. Chester had been sleeping at the foot of the bed, and now he arched his back to stretch and gave Jameson a meow greeting.

Jameson put both of his hands on Pearl's cheeks and said, "How ya doin'?"

Her speech and mobility had improved remarkably and she said, "Good. I'm good." As each day passed, Pearl's health improved and she moved easier. She could easily carry on a conversation with only slight traces of an impediment.

"I'm glad you're here," he said as he scooted down her legs onto the floor to be closer to Chester.

"Jameson," I said from the doorway, and I dragged out each syllable of his name. "You must be very careful with Aunt Pearl, okay? Good morning, Pearl. I'm just going to fix some breakfast. Would you like to come out to the kitchen table while I get things ready?"

Pearl limped into the kitchen and sat at her place. I put down the plates and a handful of flatware in front of her. She looked up at me rather puzzled. "I know, I know," I said, "you're our guest, but this is a practical exercise for you." She smiled and set the table.

"Aunt Pearl," Jameson said as he climbed onto her lap, "will it be okay to sit here when I'm four?"

"You'll be welcome on my lap as long as you fit! But, you know, you'll always fit in my heart," she told him. "Do you have a book for me to read to you? What do you have?"

He liked *The Three Little Kittens,* especially now that Chester was staying with us. Jameson opened the cardboard picture book and pointed to the words as she read.

At the conclusion of the book, she said to him, "I think when you turn four you'll be ready for longer books—for bigger boys!" And she showed him one that would be just right. Each day we could read one chapter, and you'll have to remember all about it until the next time we read. Could you do that?"

He gave her one exaggerated nod and began to slide down her legs. He was ready to go outside and play.

"Mama, can Paulie come over here to play?" he asked.

"Sure, I'll call Miss Penelope for you," I answered.

"Bye, hon! I'm leaving for Three M. See you about four o'clock!" Tom yelled. "Hey, Persnick, how about a game of hopscotch later?"

"Righto!" Pearl yelled back.

The kids were out back playing, so Pearl and I relocated to the back porch and settled on the wicker furniture. With a cup of tea to sip on, we were nice and relaxed. Cathy was swinging and singing a song she'd made up; the boys were in the sandbox. It was hot, and the sky was clear with an occasional cloud.

"Pearl? I've been wondering about some things. Why did you keep the general store?" I asked.

"Oh, just to keep busy, I suppose. When I closed the store, I put it in your name. It's yours now. You can sell it, reopen it, make it something else, whatever you like. It's in a good section of town."

"Wow! I had no idea. You just keep surprising me. Wait until I tell Tom. He'll have an idea or two," I said.

"Yes, I'm sure he will. Just remember that the building is yours."

"All right. I promise. Another question? Why do you go to the cemetery every morning?"

"The cemetery is where the office of Powwow Trust is. Did you notice the greenhouse? Well, I have a desk, a telephone, an electric typewriter, and a filing cabinet in there. I'm very good at disguising things as you may have noticed, myself included. Especially at Pearl's Gate. And if local people want to think I'm going there to be around Willow, that's fine."

"You're kidding! That's where Powwow is? Well, is there a reason why there aren't headstones for Willow and Mr. Morgan?" I asked.

"There most certainly is, and I'll tell you the shortened version. When Willow and Michael's father drowned and the bodies were found, I never saw the bodies. Michael looked familiar to me although I'd never met him, and when he told me his story—and his name—I knew that he was my nephew and that his father was my twin brother, Earl. Yes, my maiden name was Morgan. He told me that his father had a really bad gambling habit, that his grandparents—my parents—refused to help him financially any longer, and he was being hunted by a man who had loaned him money and wanted it paid back. I think they call it a loan shark. Earl's whole purpose in coming to Fiddyment was to ask Willow and me to care for Michael. We knew to watch for the man and sure enough, about three years later, he showed up in Fiddyment one day asking questions of everybody. He came into the general store and talked to me and told me that he was looking for a man named Earl Morgan and his son. I took him to the cemetery and showed him the unmarked graves. I told him that two people had drowned that day, but nobody knew them or recognized them, so it must be the father and son. That satisfied him, and he left and never came back. And that's when Michael went off to war."

I listened intently. What an amazing woman, and what an incredible story she had kept to herself all these years. She always gave me so much to think about.

"Oh my," Pearl said. "Looks like a storm is brewing. Look at those clouds..."

As soon as the words were out of her mouth, the sky turned an eerie, strange green, and the clouds were black and heavy, like dark damask cloth. Lightning bolts pierced through the darkness off in the distance. Nothing stirred, there was no breeze, no movement of the leaves in the trees. It felt like a vacuum. I went out to the yard and scanned the sky.

"I don't like this," I commented. "Let's go down to the storm cellar. Pearl?"

Pearl had gone inside to open the east and west windows in the house. I threw open the storm cellar doors and called the kids. Cathy and Paulie came running, and Pearl made it down the porch stairs. Now the wind began to whip around furiously and out of the corner of my eye, I could see a wide tornado funnel approaching. Lightning flashed all around it, and thunder roared.

"Jameson! Jameson, come here *now!* Jameson, where are you? Pearl, go down with the kids. There's a kerosene lantern down there, and matches and a transistor radio. You'll be safe. Jameson! *Jameson!* Oh, my God! Where can he be?" I yelled and looked frantically around the yard. I clutched my stomach. I felt nauseous with worry and fear.

Pearl stood on one of the stairs, beckoning me in. I was outside on the edge and told her to go down. I had to find Jameson. I closed the doors to the storm cellar and looked up. Whirling clouds looked like the underbelly of a giant alien spaceship. The sky was pitch-black with dirt and tiny particles, and filled with splintered wood being carried on the wind currents. It slammed against me, went up my nose and into my eyes. It felt like a million needles pricking my skin.

The wind was so strong I could hardly stand up, and I knew it wanted me for its very own. The wind was so loud I knew I could not be heard. The wind had such force it was sucking things into the widening funnel. It was wrapped in rain and hail, backlit by the sun, and reached from the massive smoldering clouds to the ground. I went back into the house to see if Jameson was there. Just as I closed the kitchen door, my big oak tree uprooted and hurled away from the yard. Vehicles were being tossed through the sky like confetti, a debris cloud was adding more and more dust and rubble to itself as it traveled and circled around and around ferociously. The swing set vanished before my eyes. Where was Jameson? I retreated to an interior cedar closet away from windows and crumpled to a squat on the floor among the winter coats. Tears streamed down my cheeks, I rocked back and forth on my haunches, and my brain screamed over and over, *Oh, my God, where is Jameson? Where is he? Where could he be?* I could feel the house shake and shudder. I prayed for Pearl and the children in the storm cellar and wondered if they were hearing what I heard. Things loudly crashed to the floor. And there was earsplitting screeching. I don't know how long I was in there. I didn't dare open the door, yet I wanted to. The roar created by the violence of the wind spinning mercilessly was deafening. And then it stopped. There was abrupt silence.

I tried to open the closet door and was only able to peek out. Something big, a roll-top desk, had been pushed in front of the closet door. I put all my weight into it and found strength from somewhere, coupled with an adrenaline rush and shoved the door as hard as I could.

"Let me out of here, you damned tornado!" I grunted through clenched teeth as I pushed several more times. "You won't hold me prisoner!" I gasped. Gradually, it began to move. I was able to inch the desk away enough that I could squeeze through the door's opening. I stood there, helplessly bewildered by the aftermath.

Again, I yelled, "Jameson? Jameson! It's okay to come out now! The storm is over. *Jameson!*" He still didn't come when I called.

I wanted to collapse, but I began to notice the devastation that the tornado left. On the lookout for my son, perhaps struggling to get free just as I had, I made my way through the house. I wiped my swollen eyes of tears. Dirt streaked my face. The dust hadn't settled and I began to cough. I was amazed that the house was still standing; I was shocked at how things from my walls and cupboards had been flung around the house. I stepped over broken glass that I recognized as my crystal set, a wedding present. As I made my way to and through the kitchen, I also saw my good china smashed into millions of shards, some large and some small. Bottles and jars had cracked open and the contents were spilling where they lay. Vinegar mixed with flour and sugar. A milk bottle had flown out of the refrigerator, and milk puddled beside the upturned kitchen table. A chair was half in/half out of the sink. A tree limb had crashed through the porch screen and the kitchen window and now rested on the sill. My mind was working in slow motion, and I noticed all this as I hurried through on my way to the storm cellar. I opened the doors and looked into the dim cellar. A slice of daylight shone in. Then I saw Cathy climbing the stairs toward me, followed by Paulie and Pearl. I hugged each one as they climbed out of the cellar. Pearl could tell I was distressed, but I didn't want to frighten the children.

"Paulie, you doing okay? Come with me, sweetie. I'll take you home to your mama. Do you know where Jameson went?" I asked him as we stepped over wreckage and tree branches. "I couldn't find him inside."

"Well, I saw him go inside, but not come out," he said. Just then Penelope came through the gate and saw us. We said to each other at the same time, "Are you all right?"

She dropped to her knees and held open her arms and Paulie ran into them.

"I'm fine, and I knew you'd take care of Paulie. My house is a mess…what about you?" Penelope said.

"Yeah, here too. The biggest thing is that I can't find Jameson," I told her.

Cathy's eyes got big and she asked, "Jameson? Where is he?"

Pearl's hands flew to her mouth and I saw her whisper, "Oh no." She looked around the yard at the chaos and brokenness, and I knew what she was thinking.

"What are you going to do?" Penelope asked.

"Well, I'm going to find him," I said, mustering every ounce of strength I had. "Penelope, the inside is full of broken glass…would you take Cathy home with you?"

"But, Mama, I want to help find Jameson too!" Cathy protested.

"Cathy, if we don't find him inside, we'll look for him outside. Then you can come, okay?" I said. She knew not to cause too much of a fuss and bravely walked off with Penelope.

Pearl and I went inside and started yelling for Jameson to come out. Pearl looked downstairs, I went upstairs. I looked in all the rooms and was now making my way toward Jameson's room. I had already checked the closet and now was looking under the bed when I heard Tom's car pull into the driveway.

He whistled when he saw the devastation as he came in.

"Hey, Persnick, everybody okay? Man, what a mess."

I was coming downstairs when I heard Pearl say to Tom, "...and we can't find Jameson."

I literally flew down the stairs into the comfort of his strong arms.

"What?" His brow furrowed and his speech was clipped. "What do you mean you can't find Jameson?" he said in disbelief. My husband, who always remained calm in the midst of calamity, was now stripped of his inner strength and had only raw, vulnerable disbelief.

"Paulie told us that he saw Jameson come into the house, but not leave. Pearl and I have looked inside the house. He just isn't here," I explained.

It only took an instant for Tom to take charge. We did as he said.

"Okay, Pearl, you stay here in case he shows up. Let's find you a place to sit. Is the phone working?" He picked it up. "Dead. Okay, we won't call you, but we'll come back soon and check in. Let's go, Lucy. Dear God, help us find our son."

As we went out the front door, I heard Pearl softly say, "Amen."

We stopped for Cathy next door. Our plan was to go around the block and talk to all the neighbors. It seemed that our house had received the worst damage from heaven's jackhammer. Before long, neighbors joined in the search for Jameson. We heard Jameson's name being echoed over and over from one block to the next. Several hours had passed since the tornado and it was getting dark. The neighbors stayed out looking for Jameson and we went home for the car. I ducked my head in to give Pearl an update.

"Pearl? You doing okay here? Want to come with us in the car?" I asked. She had begun to sweep the wreckage into a pile, but decided to come with us.

We drove toward the school and asked people along the way if they'd seen Jameson. We went to the police station to enlist their help, and gave them a description of Jameson and what he was wearing. They suggested that we go home since it was dark and get some rest, and begin again at first light.

None of us could sleep. We didn't want to be in our disarrayed bedrooms, and I didn't have the energy to try to clean them. So we cleared the living room furniture and collapsed there. The electricity had come back on and the phone was working. I listened to the television news reports about the tornado touching down in our community, and the police had released the information about Jameson missing. His picture seemed huge on the TV screen.

"A three-year-old boy has been missing from his parents' home ever since the tornado plowed through the sleepy village of Fiddyment with horrific brute force. Neighbors and community people searched for him until dark, and they will continue the search in the morning. If you happen to see Jameson Maguire, please call 555-1234. We'll keep you updated. Jameson, hang on, buddy" was the commentator's report.

The phone rang. It was Michael. They'd heard the news and were concerned and worried. We assured them that we would let them know the second we found Jameson.

I was exhausted, but I dozed on the sofa next to Tom until dawn, and like a robot, went out to the kitchen to make coffee and hot tea. Everything concerning taking care of the family was now mechanical. I stood over the sink and my entire body heaved with my sobs as I pleaded with God, "Please don't take my baby."

Pearl came and stood beside me and put her arm around my shoulders. "We'll find him," she said. "We'll find him this morning. I just know it."

We drove up Hill Street and past the church. We continued for several more blocks, then we saw a crowd gathering, and a fire truck. One fireman was climbing a ladder, leaning against a tall tree. A police car and an ambulance arrived.

"Tom? Look ahead. Let's stop, okay?" I said.

As soon as we got out of the car and joined the crowd, they began telling us about a little boy perched on a tree limb.

"Poor little thing…he looks just terrible. We think he must've gotten carried off by the tornado. What an experience! I hope he's okay," one woman said.

And then I saw him. It *was* Jameson! His clothing was filthy, tattered, and torn; he was missing a shoe and sock, and his little foot and leg hung over a limb. He had big scratches, some clawlike marks, and bruises all over his body. His skin was pitted from the dust, dirt, and debris. His curly red hair was all disheveled and almost stood straight up. But he was alive. That's all that mattered.

"Hey there, young feller, how'd you get up here?" the fireman asked as he climbed the ladder's rungs.

"The wind brought me," he said.

"The wind? Well, how'd you get in the tree?" asked the fireman, almost in disbelief. The tree didn't have low enough branches that the little boy could've climbed the tree.

"The wind dropped me up there," he said as he looked up to the top. "We fell through leaves and branches to get here. I saved the cat," he said proudly and showed him the big black cat.

Cats don't normally like to be wet or hurled through the air or feel out of control, and this one had endured a very harrowing experience and still looked scared, but was calm around Jameson.

"Yes, you did. That was very brave of you. What's your kitty's name?" the fireman asked as he got to the top.

"Chester," Jameson replied, "but he's Aunt Pearl's."

"Would you like to come down? You just stay there and let me come to you, okay?"

Jameson was straddling a tree limb and Chester was stretched out on the limb in front of him, enjoying the rays of sunshine that filtered through the tree branches. Somebody's camera flashed to capture the moment.

Before long, the fireman brought Jameson, who was holding Chester like a baby, down the ladder while we were waiting at the bottom. The crowd applauded the rescue and made lots of noise as we thanked the fireman and embraced our tornado-beaten little guy. The EMT looked Jameson over and didn't think there were any broken bones. I had more tears brimming in my eyes, but these were tears of joy. When we were all in the car, we asked Jameson to tell us the story.

"Well, Aunt Pearl went into the house, and I did too. I wanted to get Chester and I couldn't find him. He was sleeping on Aunt Pearl's chair. I put him in my arms, like this, and we went outside. I saw you, Mama, but you didn't see me. It was very, very windy. I saw the wind pick up my pail from the sandbox. Then it picked us up too. We went round and round and *waaaaay* up into the sky. I held Chester tight and closed my eyes. We were in the sky for a long time. Then the wind dropped us in the tree." His motions helped paint the picture of his harrowing experience.

"Well, sweetie," I said, "I'm so glad you and Chester are safe. Were you afraid last night?"

"Nope," Jameson answered. "Chester and me, we keeped close. This morning I saw a lady getting her newspaper and I yelled '*help!*' really loud so she could hear me. I knew you would find me. Daddy, did you and the band go for a sky ride too?"

"Sky ride? Oh. No, we didn't. We were rehearsing and marching in the field and saw the tornado coming, so we went into the school's basement. But one of our tubas—you know, the great, big brass horn—was ripped right out of the arms of Bobby Young, and it landed on top of the flagpole."

Cathy had remained quiet; now she said, "The flagpole? Could we see it?"

"Mama, I'm hungry," said Jameson.

"I bet you are! How about we stop at the drive-in, Tom? We could all use a treat after what we've been through."

The carhop brought our food and we finally relaxed a little. She had heard the story about Jameson and asked him for his autograph. I was glad I'd helped him learn his letters and how to print his name. Then, after driving by the school to see the flagpole, we made our way home.

"Well, I'll be..." Tom finished his brief story as we pulled up to our house. "Looks like a TV news crew is here."

The crew rushed out of the news van and rapidly set up cameras and microphones. The young field reporter came over to greet us and introduce herself. Then she saw Jameson.

"Oh! You found him! I love a story with a happy ending. Do you mind if we film you and ask you a few questions?" Tammy asked. "Is it okay if I ask Jameson a couple of questions?"

After the interview, she asked if we had damage to the house and backyard.

"Oh, we sure did. Would you like to see?" I asked.

The crew came into the house and out to the back porch and were amazed at what they saw. Several of the men whistled as they climbed over tipped furniture or said words like "whew" and "oh my gosh." There was a big, deep hole where the tree had been, and things from other people's homes and yards had been dumped into ours. We showed them the storm cellar and the closet where I stayed.

"This will be on the six o'clock news tonight!" Tammy yelled as the van pulled away.

"Tom, maybe you should take Pearl over to her house to see how she fared. I'll stay here and bathe Jameson and do some clean-up," I said.

"Good idea, Luce. What do you think, Persnick? Shall we go?" he asked Pearl. "C'mon, Cathy!"

As they drove to Pearl's house, they could see the path the tornado made. With no rhyme or reason, it cut through homes, yards, streets, toward the creek, then veered off through a field toward the next town. As they got to the top of Pearl's driveway, they were totally surprised. There stood her charming cottage home, totally unscathed and unblemished. The tornado totally sidestepped it. Then they headed for Pearl's Gate and Powwow Trust.

Chapter 8

Pearl took Tom and Cathy into Pearl's Gate through another disguised back entrance closer to the greenhouse. Even though Tom had lived in Fiddyment most of his life, he had no idea that this little hidden cemetery existed, much less Powwow Trust. It was obvious that the tornado hadn't even come to this part of town, but Pearl wanted to go into Powwow and pull Lucy's files so they could go over them later.

The office of Powwow Trust was inside a nondescript greenhouse in the rear corner of the cemetery, and it appeared to be connected to a wooden shed. The entire building was made of glass and steel support beams. All the windows of the greenhouse were dirty, and the sun sifted in through the smudges. There were many beautiful hanging plants and flowers, and others lined up on shelves inside. A misting system was in place, and in one corner was a mish-mash of gardening tools. Everything thrived because of the humidity, and it gave off the feel and aroma of a tropical rain forest. If somebody happened by and peeked in the windows, they wouldn't even be curious. In the back was a doorway into the wooden shed, and it would be assumed that it was more of the same. But that's where Powwow was located. There was even a six-foot tall wooden Indian guarding the doorway and a sign over it that said

POWWOW. Michael had hand-carved the life-sized Indian statue, which was wearing a highly detailed leather-fringed shirt and pants, a red sash tied around his waist. The Indian also wore a carved and painted turquoise necklace, and his head was decorated with two feathers. Two braids hung down his shoulders, and he wore moccasins. Cathy noticed him right away and asked Pearl if he had a name.

"Yes, he does. It's Chief Wampum," Pearl said.

"Wampum, eh?" Tom remarked. He chuckled to himself. "Very clever, Persnick." He saw the puzzled look on Cathy's face and said, "It's an Indian word that means money," which was enough to satisfy the curiosity forming in her head.

"Let's take one of these hanging baskets home to Lucy. She could use a pick-me-up. Cathy? Do you see a plant you'd like for your bedroom?" Pearl asked as she unhooked a huge Boston fern.

Cathy pointed to a small pot filled with purple flowers. "Beautiful. It's called African violet, and I would've chosen that very plant myself."

While they were gone, I bathed Jameson and tended to his scratches. I could tell that Chester hadn't enjoyed the "sky ride" very much, and the evidence was on Jameson's chest and back. There was one place on his forearm that looked like a teeny pebble was stuck, so I put a strip of tape on it, then ripped the tape off. Sure enough, the pebble stuck to the tape.

"Wow, Mama! How'd you do that?" Jameson asked excitedly.

"Oh, just Mama knowledge," I told him. "Jameson, until we get the house all cleaned up, you must always wear shoes, all right? I wouldn't want you stepping on broken glass. How about coloring at the kitchen table while I tackle the kitchen?"

"Okay," Jameson agreed.

By the time the gang came back, I had managed to clean the kitchen of large debris, make a grocery list, and straighten Pearl's room. Several things in Pearl's room had fallen to the floor but didn't break. The magazines were easy to restack and the clothes were easy to pick up from the closet floor. Her bed moved about six inches and I shoved it back into place. Poor Chester was all tuckered out and with one swift movement he was on the sunny windowsill and stretched out for a catnap. Jameson wandered in while I straightened up and was now napping on Pearl's bed.

Cathy saw me first, and I put my index finger to my lips to tell her to speak softly and then I joined them in the kitchen. Pearl put the kettle on to make tea, and I asked about the status of her house.

"Oh, fine. You couldn't even tell a twister came through," she said.

"And Powwow?" I asked.

"The same. Everything at Pearl's Gate is fine. But we stopped into Powwow and I have some files to show you later on," Pearl said.

Tom came in carrying two boxes and the Boston fern. The lower box had files in it; the top one held a couple of plants.

"Mmmmm, these are very nice," I commented.

"This one is for you, m'dear…just something pretty for a sunny spot," said Pearl as she held out the fern. "I think it would like the back porch, and Cathy personally selected the African violet for her room."

"Yeah, and Mama, wait until you see Chief Wampum!" said Cathy. "He's neat."

Tom came back into the kitchen and said that he'd called the insurance company and they would send an appraiser over to see what we could replace and also check on structural damage.

"Mama, is it okay if I go upstairs and see my room?" Cathy asked.

"Sure, just be careful," I answered.

She took her African violet with her and came back down in a few minutes.

"Just some things fell off my dresser and bookcase, and I put them back on top," she told us. "Can we paint my room purple to match the violets?" she asked.

"Sure. Ready for a change, are you?" I said as I winked.

Chapter 9

During the afternoon and evening, we managed to get the inside of the house pretty much cleaned up and safe. The outside was a different matter and like Tara in *Gone with the Wind*, we'd think about that tomorrow. After the kids were in bed, Pearl, Tom, and I sat around the kitchen table and looked at the various files and discussed what everything meant. There were T-bills, stocks, bonds, mutual funds, certificates, life insurance policies, checkbooks, savings account statements, papers on purchases and sales, deeds, information about various safe deposit boxes, and my mother's will. It was a lot to take in and digest.

"Without an adding machine, I'd say you're worth several million dollars," said Pearl.

"Several…million?" I questioned and gulped at the same time. "Are you sure?"

"Oh my, yes. The money I sent when you were in college was just the interest from one of the investments," Pearl said.

"Well, what do I do with it?" I asked.

"Invest it to make more, be a philanthropist, travel, start a business, go shopping, whatever you like," Pearl told us. "Just be careful and wise with it. When you have wealth like this, God expects you to be responsible."

"I've been thinking about ways to improve Fiddyment, to make it more inviting and attractive to our residents and neighboring communities. Is that something I could do with some of my money?" I asked.

"Yes, of course. And I think that's a grand idea," said Pearl. "Do you have any specific ideas?"

"Well, I'd encourage business owners to take more pride of ownership and spiffy up their shops to make them appealing for visitors, develop a play area for the children, donate some money to the church and to the music program at the high school, put more welcome signage outside of town, and, Tom, I haven't even mentioned this to you, but I'd like to do something with the old general store…be an example to everyone else," I suggested.

"Sounds good, Luce. Would you revisit the general store or do something else?" Tom asked.

"Oh, I don't know…not yet anyway. I'll start thinking about it. First, we have to make some repairs in the house and the backyard. What should we do with that huge hole where the tree was?" I asked both of them.

"We can fill it in and put another bush of some kind there," Tom said.

"A swimming pool would improve your property value," Pearl suggested. "You could put an attractive, tall fence around it to be safe and to keep inquisitive neighbors out."

"The kids love to swim. Thinking ahead, if we made a fun place for them to invite friends over, we'll have better control over them when they're teens," I said. "What do you think, Tom?"

"I think a pool costs a lot of money to install and upkeep," Tom said.

I held up the files on the table and just looked at him.

"Oh yeah, I forgot. Wow, it hasn't sunk in yet," Tom said. "I wouldn't mind having a pool."

"Well, let's sleep on it and talk about it again tomorrow," I said as I yawned. "I'm absolutely bushed."

The next morning, we were all back in the kitchen having breakfast when the doorbell rang. It was Michael and his family with clean-up equipment and a bag of doughnuts.

"Reporting for duty, sir," Michael said as he saluted in the doorway.

Michael looked at Jameson and said, "Hey, there Twister…how ya doing?" and Jameson made a mad dash toward Michael and leaped into his arms.

"Hey, come on in. It's so good to see you," Tom said as he slapped Michael on the back. "You came to give us a hand? That's pretty amazing."

"Uh, you're family. Families help each other," Michael said. "Looks like you've made headway in here. What about out back?"

"That's a different story. I've ordered a dumpster which should be delivered any time," Tom told him and they went out the door to the back porch.

We spent the morning cleaning up—sweeping, vacuuming, sorting, washing, and polishing. The guys, and Abby and Gabby, worked outside hauling debris and putting it in one pile. And then we heard it. The dumpster was delivered to the strains of "76 Trombones" while the high school band marched down the sidewalk two by two and stopped in front of our place and finished the tune. The kids weren't in their uniforms, but they still had pride and they looked and sounded fabulous.

The drum major marched forward toward Tom and said, "We came to help, Mr. Maguire. What can we do for you?"

Tom was dumbfounded and stood there speechless. Finally, Michael said to Tom, "The dumpster is here; why not have the kids fill it?"

So they did.

Late in the afternoon, the marching band left and we were settling down. Michael and Gail said to us in unison, "We have an idea. How about we take the kids home with us for a couple of days? We'll go to the museum, to the lake, out for pizza, to the zoo. Then you guys and Aunt Pearl could come for the kids and stay for the weekend. We've got plenty of room, Abby and Gabby would love to oversee playtime with your kiddles, and we've got a guesthouse for you, Tom and Lucy. What do you think about that?"

All four children looked at us anxiously waiting for a reply.

Tom and I looked at each other and at Pearl; we all shrugged our shoulders and in unison said, "Great."

After our children left with the Morgans and the house was quiet, Pearl and I sat out on the back porch looking over the changes in the yard.

"I miss the tree," I commented. "It gave us some good shade."

"Well," said Pearl, "I've been sitting here visualizing a swimming pool, and you know, Lucy, it's a perfect spot. You've got plenty of room to put in a good-sized pool and maybe even an attached Jacuzzi. You could even have a shallow end for little tykes and non-swimmers."

I could sense her excitement and I became interested. "Do you think there's room for a cabana out there?" I asked.

"Oh, sure," she said. "That would be nice for guests to change out of their wet clothes without going inside the house."

Tom started the barbeque to grill steaks for us, and we knew he couldn't hear our discussion, but he yelled in our direction, "I think a pool would be great out here!"

That confirmed it. We were getting a pool.

Chapter 10

The Morgans gave us directions to their home in Lake Forest via Chicago's Lake Shore Drive. That way, we avoided the elevated train, called "the el," and city traffic. We passed Buckingham Fountain and its summer-time visitors before turning north. It was a glorious day, and the harbor and lake were dotted with lots of colorful sailboats. The lake was the color of turquoise and blue sapphires, and you almost could not tell where the sky met the water on the horizon. As we drove on the outskirts of the "Windy City," we were aware of the spectacular skyline, and we began to see the homes across the street from the shore. Many were three-story stately homes with big fenced yards, and originally for carriages, a covered area over the driveway beside the homes to protect passengers from the weather before the driver moved the car into the five to ten-car garage. Gardeners tended to the lawns, shrubbery, and flower gardens. Everything looked absolutely perfect.

"We're almost there," Pearl said. "Turn left at the next light."

The final turn was onto Lakeside Lane. Trees were lined up along the curbs on both sides of the street and formed a thick canopy. Pearl pointed to Michael's house.

"There it is," she said.

Tom whistled. Their home was one of the historic estate homes built in the late 1800s, and Michael and Gail had restored it to its original charm. The drive circled in front of the huge home.

We stopped at the closed gate and Tom pushed a button.

"Who's calling please?" a deep voice said.

"Uh, the Maguires," said Tom.

"Drive forward and park at the side please," the voice said and then giggled.

I couldn't wait to see the inside of the house.

As soon as we parked, the door opened and the kids all hurried out to help us with our things.

"Hey, Gabby, was that you answering the doorbell?" Tom asked as he held Gabby in a headlock and ruffled his auburn hair.

Abby and Gabby took our luggage to the guesthouse on the other side of the rear garden and then hurried back to the main house.

"Hi, Aunt Pearl!" said Cathy and Jameson. They both gave her a big kiss on the cheek.

"Your room is in here," Jameson continued. "Gail said you would be tomtorf…comtorf…" and he stopped, stomped his foot, and crossed his arms. "What's that word?" he whispered loudly to Cathy.

"Comfortable, Jameson. Com-fort-a-ble. Remember?" said Cathy. She had an irritating edge to her voice.

"Yes, indeed I will be comfortable," said Pearl. "I've had my own room here ever since they bought this house. Want to see it, Lucy?"

"Absolutely. Lead the way," I answered.

Before we got to her room, Pearl showed us the gourmet kitchen, the butler's pantry, a beautiful family room, the formal living room which overlooked the lake, the formal dining room, the library, the music room, Michael's home office, and two of the four fireplaces. That was just the main floor and didn't even cover the wings on either side. The house had three stories with dormers in the top floor; it was sprawling, comfortable, and tastefully decorated, but not opulent.

"I thought my house was big," I muttered to myself during the tour.

"Well, sometimes large homes are necessary," Pearl said. "Michael does a lot of entertaining of clients and friends. He's on the board of directors for several non-profit organizations and they hold their annual board meetings here… and things like that. There are eight bedrooms and each has its own bath. There are three half-baths, and there are three bedrooms and two sofa beds in the guesthouse."

Pearl's room was exquisite but looked like her. It was warm and inviting. The room had a French antique bed which beckoned "come hither" and was covered by a white satin, fluffy, down comforter, and there was a white quilt with various shades of pink roses folded at the foot of the bed. Other antiques were thoughtfully placed around the room. A tall armoire stood majestically against one wall. A huge white fluffy rug adorned the mahogany hardwood floor.

"Who made the quilt, Pearl?" I asked.

"My mother did. Isn't it lovely?" Pearl answered.

I went over to examine the work. "My, my, my, the stitches are absolutely perfect," I said. "And the quilting is fabulous!"

"Hi, there!" Gail said as she rushed in. Their golden retriever, Taffy, was with her, wagging her tail and anxious to meet the new people. "I figured Pearl would be giving you the grand tour." She embraced both of us. "I hope you haven't worried about the kids. Your children are so well behaved, Lucy. It's been a joy to have them here. But I'll let them tell you the stories. Let's go out to the garden and have some tea and scones, all right?"

The three of us moved down the hallway while Gail pointed out various paintings and décor changes she had made. She was quite the interior designer.

We went through beveled glass-paned French doors to the backyard from the kitchen. The patio was partially shaded by an overhead trellis covered with climbing flowering plants; the patio had been beautifully and tastefully decorated with furniture—an outdoor dining table and matching chairs—which we learned had been made by Michael. There were several steps down to the pool and several lounge chairs around it.

Gail talked about the various things they had done to restore their home, and I couldn't imagine it any other way than it now stood.

"Lucy, Pearl," Gail said between sips of hot tea, "would you be at all interested in riding into town with me? I need to stop by the butcher shop, and I could show you around a little. In fact, let's make this a girls' afternoon and leave the kiddles and the men here to fend off intruders," Gail said.

"Do you think they're up to it?" I asked. "Fending off intruders, I mean?"

"Oh sure. They can fight the Vikings and then swim with the kids and have a good time without us here," Gail said.

She approached Michael and told him our plans, and he smiled and told us to have a good time.

We piled into their car, a shiny new midnight-blue Cadillac, and headed to town. As we drove along, Gail told us about the sights as we passed them. She explained that they had chosen Lake Forest for several reasons—because of its charm, location (close to downtown Chicago and the lake), and they had fallen in love with the house. Lake Forest was a very affluent community and when it was first developed, the general concept reflected in the plan was of a city in a park, with its picturesque streets laid out in such a manner that it took into account such natural features as the ravines and lake bluffs, instead of forcing the street plan into a formal grid. She explained to us that several long-time residents had been meeting to form a land conservation organization and purchase open space in the interest of preserving animal habitat, restoring ecosystems, and providing environmental education for the city's children. Since I was interested in beautifying Fiddyment, I was eager to learn all I could.

The business area was charming, quaint, and clean. Parking was at a diagonal; the streets and sidewalks were in good repair. There were well cared for plants hanging from the old-fashioned armed street lights, many of the shops had clever names; many had colorful awnings over the doorway, and all the shops had something inviting at the front door; the window displays were beautifully arranged. There were park benches to rest on and visit with other folks while waiting for a shopper, and the French bakery gave away free doughnut holes when a dozen doughnuts were purchased; two small tables and chairs were out in front for patrons to have a cup of coffee and a French sweet treat. People were warm and friendly and seemed to know everyone by name.

"Well, I must say," said Lucy as she snapped pictures with her camera, "this is delightful and gives me some good ideas for Fiddyment. I think it'll be a fun project, don't you, Pearl?"

"Yes, I do. I'd even like to donate some of the plants I know you're thinking about, if you don't mind," answered Pearl. "Between my garden and yours, and the greenhouse, we can add a little color to downtown Fiddyment."

"You might think about an open-air market," Gail suggested. "That's always a big draw around here. It's held on Saturday mornings during the summer. Or an autumn craft fair at the square! I bet there's some great creative talent in Fiddyment. Ah. Here's the Meat Grinder."

We went into the butcher shop and Gail asked for ribs; the plan was to marinate them overnight and then bake them until they fell off the bone. We women would make the side dishes and have a good old Southern-style feast.

"If we get some buttermilk, I'll make us a buttermilk pie," Pearl said.

"You're on!" Gail said. "That is definitely one of your specialties, Pearl, and it just isn't made around here."

We paused in front of a children's clothing store. I chuckled at its name. It was called Too Big for My Britches. Then Gail pointed to a building across the street. One of the businesses was a restaurant, The Lantern, which looked like it belonged in the French Quarter. It had white-washed brick and wrought-iron rails on either side of the entrance, and a window box with geraniums at the base of the window. Small paned windows allowed us to see the tables inside. A chalkboard menu was posted on the door. Basically, it was a friendly, neighborhood restaurant for the locals.

"That's one of our favorite places, and we're taking everyone there for dinner tonight," Gail told us. "I'm sure you'll love it."

When we got home, the kids were just getting out of the pool, and Michael and Tom were already dressed and lounging on the patio.

"Hey, girls, have fun?" Michael asked. "And, yes, I made reservations for six thirty. I told them you were coming, Aunt Pearl, and you know what they want."

"Oh, my…I don't know if I'm up for that," Pearl said.

"Up for what?" I asked.

"No! Don't tell them," Gail said. "Let's make it a surprise! Have you even been back to the guesthouse? Let me take you. Is it okay if Abby helps your kiddles get dressed and ready?"

With that, the surprise was forgotten and Gail took us to the guesthouse. As I expected, it was charming inside and out, and decorated like an English cottage. The living and dining rooms shared a cathedral ceiling and a fireplace. Tall windows framed the living room fireplace. A pass-through joined the dining room to the combination kitchen and family room, which featured a snack bar and a window. There was a separate sleeping wing which had a master suite, a skylight in the dressing area, and a luxurious bath. The den, or third bedroom, shared a second full bath with another bedroom. Each room had been painstakingly decorated.

"Wow," I whispered after Gail left. "This feels so comfortable. I halfway expect Prince Charming to come through the door."

"Well, here I am," Tom said and he kissed me tenderly.

We were dozing when the phone rang.

"Maguire's Summer Home. Some are here. Some are not," Tom answered in an Irish brogue.

There was silence. Then, "I think I must have…wait a minute. Tom? Is that you?" Michael asked. "Maguire's Summer Home? Man…where did *that* come from?" he said as he chuckled. These two men had become good friends in such a short time.

"Oh, I don't know," Tom answered.

"Gail wanted me to let you know that she made appetizers, and you can come back over to the main house any time, but we'll be leaving at six o'clock. And we'll need to take both cars."

The Lantern had a lit oil lantern hanging outside, little white twinkle lights around the windows fringed with French fabric curtains, and candles already glowed on each table. The inside was decorated in the style of an old country French home. Simon, the maître d', greeted them at the door.

"Ah, good evening, Morgan family and friends. How nice to see you this evening. Your table is ready. Please follow me," he said in a velvety British accent. "Miss Pearl," he continued, "how are you this evening?"

"I'm very well, Simon. Thank you for asking," she said as he seated her. "I always enjoy coming here."

The food and service were quite good. At the end of the meal, the owner came over to greet us and whispered something to Pearl. She dabbed the corner of her mouth with the napkin and stood. He escorted her to a little stage area and she sat behind a hammered dulcimer set on a stand at an angle. Pearl picked up the mallets and began to play. Delightful sweet strains of anything she played wafted from the dulcimer. Jameson looked at me, wide-eyed and lips formed a perfect O. He climbed onto my lap for a better view.

"Mama," Cathy whispered into my ear, "that's beautiful. What's it called? I want to learn to play that. Could I? Could I, Mama?"

The restaurant that used to be abuzz with conversation and platter clatter was now quiet. Everyone paid attention.

Everyone listened. Everyone loved it. I could hear folks seated close to me whispering about how beautiful it was.

After fifteen minutes or so, Pearl finished. The restaurant owner went to her and thanked her for giving them the gift of beautiful music and escorted her back to her seat amid enthusiastic applause.

"Well, Aunt Pearl, you've still got it," Michael said. "That was something else. Next time I'll bring my autoharp and we can play as we used to on the front porch. Is everyone finished? Gail has dessert at home so we can leave whenever you're ready."

"Pearl, that was an incredible surprise," I said. "I knew that you played the dulcimer, but I've never heard one. And now you even have Cathy interested!"

"Cathy with a C, is that true? Would you like to learn to play?" Pearl asked Cathy.

"Oh yes," Cathy whispered, still mesmerized.

"Then I'll teach you," Pearl said.

We were all in the kitchen back at the Morgan home. Gail made coffee, I cut slices from a three-layer chocolate cake, and Pearl was in charge of the ice cream and scoop. We had decided to have dessert and then play Monopoly in teams. We were just putting everything on the table when the doorbell rang.

Michael went to the door. We could hear him greet whoever it was.

"Jeff, you old son-of-a-gun," Michael said as he slapped his back. "How are you? Come on in. We were just having dessert."

"Everyone, this is my old friend and board-sitting colleague, Jeff Easterbrook."

The Morgan family was very happy to see him. Even Taffy barked her greeting and jumped onto his legs.

Introductions were made and he went around shaking hands, chatting a little with everyone; he was very charming and had a friendly way with people.

Jefferson Davis Easterbrook was a tall, well-built man. He had white wavy hair, a mustache, dark brown eyes, and a toothy smile that was contagious. His skin was leathery and tanned from being outdoors. He spoke with a Southern drawl, and his voice was rich and deep. Tonight he wore a white shirt, jeans, a jacket, and Western boots.

"Pearl Morgan…I remember you," he said when he got to Pearl. He held both her hands in his.

"I'm sorry," she said, looking puzzled as she withdrew her hands from his. "Have we met? I have been Pearl Witsche for many years now."

"Aunt Pearl and my dad were twins," Michael told him.

"Yes, yes, I remember," Jeff said. "Well, Pearl, I visited your home in Virginia when I was much younger. I had business with your father. I believe you were being courted by Willowby Witsche, and I'm afraid he beat me to you."

"Yes, he did," Pearl replied and looked straight into his eyes.

"Please, Jeff, have a seat. Have you had dinner?" Michael asked. "Gabby, will you go grab a chair from the dining room please?"

"No, no, I'm fine, thank you. We ate on the plane, but that cake looks awfully good," he said. "I've never been one to turn down chocolate." He sat at the table and crossed his long legs at the ankles.

"How are things in Kentucky?" Michael asked.

"Grand. The farm is doing nicely. I've got two horses that are ready to race." He looked at the group. "I breed thoroughbred race horses," he told them.

"I love horses," Jameson piped in.

"You know, Jameson, you look like a little boy I saw on television that was carried off by a tornado recently," said Jeff.

"Yup, that was me," Jameson proudly said. "Me and Chester—that's Aunt Pearl's cat—we went for a sky ride."

"Wow. That must've been some ride. But if you love horses, you'll have to come to my farm and see mine. Maybe Armando would let you ride with him," he suggested. "At least you'd be a little lower to the ground," he said as he winked at me.

"Would anyone like more cake?" Gail asked.

"No, thanks, but I'll have half a cup of coffee please." Jefferson waited while Gail poured, then stood and went over to the vanilla ice cream, got a big scoop and plopped it into his coffee.

"I see the Monopoly game out and ready. Are you going to play? May I join you?" Jeff asked.

"Yes, we are, and yes, you may!" said Michael.

"Wonderful!" Jeff responded. "If we play in teams, might I play with Abby and Jameson? We'll probably beat you, so get ready for a fight, right, Abby? Jameson, come over here and sit on my lap so you can tell me what to do."

The game got wild with one team arguing, another loudly flaunting their purchases, another team pulling ahead with houses and hotels, and then the next team would buy a railroad. I spent quite a bit of time in jail. Jeff was very good to include Jameson in a decision being made and let him choose house or hotel tiles to put out on the board.

"All right, all right," Michael announced sadly to the group, "my team is bankrupt. I believe Jeff and company have won the game fair and square. Do you all agree?"

"Yeah," the kids grumbled.

"Then I pronounce this game of Monopoly finished!" Michael said. "Abby and Gabby, will you put Cathy and Jameson to bed please? We'll see you all in the morning!" After much ado of saying goodnight amid hugs and kisses, all four children left the room.

Gail came back from the kitchen carrying a tray with brandy and brandy snifters.

"So, what brings you to the North?" Michael asked Jeff.

Each person found a comfortable seat, and they fell into a conversation about Jeff's visit to Chicago.

Jeff spoke slowly and deliberately as he recalled the story he was telling, and we could tell the memories were very vivid for him.

"Six weeks ago Armando's daughter and granddaughter went into town on an errand and were driving back to the farm. There was a terrible accident right where the main road and the driveway to Easterbrook Farms intersect. The car hit something, rolled over several times, and blew up. Armando and I were in the stables and heard the explosion. We got in the truck and drove to the site and were the first to find them. His daughter was ejected through the windshield and we found her in the field. She died at the scene. We were able to pull Tessa, his eleven-year-old granddaughter, from the car, but she suffered horrible third-degree burns and has been in and out of the hospital. There is a special burn unit here and they want to do a skin graft," he told us. "I would hope that she can look normal some day. Right now the scarring is just…it will take time and many, many surgeries." He stopped for a moment before he continued. "I can't begin to imagine how much the medical bills must be. But I want to help. The first graft is Monday morning, and I want to be there with Armando. He shouldn't be alone while he waits."

The story of the accident and Tessa, and the way he told it, stabbed me in the heart. Gail, Pearl, and I all had tears in our eyes.

"Do you think there was foul play?" Michael asked.

"Well, in my line of business, there are always jealous competitors and scoundrels, and my horses are well known in the racing world, so there is a police investigation," Jeff answered.

We were all quiet for several moments thinking about the things he had told us.

"By the way, Jeff, if you have hotel reservations, please cancel them. You're welcome to stay here with us for as long as you need," Michael said. "We have plenty of room."

At first Jeff didn't say anything. "Thank you, Michael… Gail…your hospitable offer is graciously accepted. It's so much nicer to be around caring people like yourselves. I'll be here for a couple of days, then I'll need to get back to the farm. And Armando will be staying at the hospital."

"Besides money for medical bills, is there anything else Armando needs?" Michael asked.

"Well, I'm sure in the back of his brain he's worrying about raising Tessa, but getting her better is the main thing," Jeff answered.

"I can't speak for the others, but Gail and I would certainly like to help. Perhaps we could start a trust fund," Michael said.

The rest of us—Pearl, Tom, and I—all agreed that we would like to participate too. I had wondered how I would enter the world of philanthropy, and this was new to me, helping in such a way. But, as Pearl had told me, with wealth comes responsibility. This was definitely a worthy cause. Pearl smiled at me proudly.

The next morning, the guesthouse phone rang. It was Michael telling us that all the kiddles were making breakfast and it would be ready in forty-five minutes. He was taking Taffy for a walk and invited us to go with him. We did. He told us that he and Jeff had both been up early and discussed the possibilities of what we may be able to do.

"He's an interesting, charming man," I said. "Does he have family?"

"No, he never married. I asked him about it several years ago, and he told me that he was too busy and involved in his work to have room for a family. Too much stuff on his plate, he said. I think he's made us his unofficial family because whenever he's in Chicago, he drops in on us. We love seeing him and having him around. We always invite him to come up for the holidays but he never has. Maybe this year. Listen, I wanted to mention some things to the two of you about this particular philanthropic endeavor. Okay?" Michael proceeded to explain some of the things we would have to do and what the group would do to form a trust fund for Tessa.

"Okay, Taffy, let's go home," Michael said, and Taffy sprinted ahead of us.

You could feel the energy in the kitchen and breakfast room. Abby and Gabby were making French toast, bacon, and scrambled eggs; Cathy was setting the table; Gail was dicing fresh fruit; Pearl and Jefferson were sipping coffee and occupied in conversation.

"I'm really sorry to hear that I didn't make a lasting impression on you," Jeff said.

"Well, I never said that, Jefferson Easterbrook," she retorted. "I only agreed that I was being courted by Willowby and you were too late. When I heard your name,

I knew exactly who you were, but I never expected to run into you at my nephew's home after all these years."

"And tell me, Madame, what have you done with yourself all these years hence?" Jeff asked.

"Why do you want to know?" she rebutted, but she also smiled. I noticed that her eyes sparkled.

"Simply curious catch-up conversation," he replied.

"Oh, I kept busy with Willow and the general store until he passed, then I ran it alone and discovered that I was good at running businesses. Even started another store in a neighboring town. Michael lived with me after Earl and Willow drowned, and he helped out at the store until he joined the army. I watched out for Lucy from afar after her mama died, and we just reconnected earlier this summer. You can probably tell that the Maguires are like family to me, and that's a good thing because I stayed with them after I had a stroke, and I'm just now feeling ready to go back home."

"Breakfast is served," Abby said as she came into the room and put a platter of French toast on the table. Gabby followed her with platters of crispy bacon and scrambled eggs.

"What are everyone's plans for today?" Jeff asked.

"I'm making a pie right after breakfast," Pearl answered.

"Oh, really?" asked Abby, her interest piqued. "May I help you, Aunt Pearl?"

"Yes, you may," Pearl said.

"I'm getting the ribs ready for the oven," Gail said, "then…I don't know. We hadn't made any definite plans."

"We have to go home this evening or in the morning," Tom said. "I've got a marching band rehearsal tomorrow afternoon."

Jeff looked surprised.

"Marching band? Are you the conductor?" Jeff wanted to know.

"Yes, I am. And the science teacher at Fiddyment High. The band is really good this year, and we'll show our competition a thing or two at the football games," Tom said.

"Ah, there's nothing like a high school football game on a chilly autumn evening," Jeff said. "How far is Fiddyment from here? Maybe I could go to a game with you on one of my trips here."

"You are always welcome at our place, Jeff. So I'll send you the schedule of our home games so you know how to plan," Tom replied.

"Wonderful!" Jeff said. "I'm going to go to the hospital a little later. Would any of you care to come with me? Armando would be happy for the company, I'm sure."

Chapter 11

Pearl and Gail decided to stay home with the kids and begin food preparations. Pearl gathered all the ingredients for her buttermilk pie and called Abby to the kitchen. Together, they made two pie crusts for their creations. The rest of us went with Jeff to the hospital.

Armando was in Tessa's room and he happily greeted Jeff.

"*Señor* Jeff! It is so good of you to come. Look, Tessa… Señor Jeff has come to visit," Armando said.

Tessa raised one gauze-wrapped hand. Her hands had been severely burned and the hospital staff had been trying to protect them from amputation. Her face had huge, deep gashes angling from her left eyebrow to the right side of her chin. Much of her hair had been singed off. Tessa's spirits were good, and she gazed gratefully at Jeff.

Armando and Jeff shook hands and Jeff stood with one hand on Armando's broad shoulders.

"Tom, Lucy, I'd like you to meet Armando Vasquez, the best horse trainer in North America. He's a horse whisperer if I've ever seen one. Armando is originally from Argentina and he brought his family here to work with me and my horses. Armando, these are my new friends, Tom and Lucy Maguire. I believe you have met Michael Morgan."

Tom and I shook Armando's hand.

"Oh. And, of course, Tessa, who is having surgery tomorrow morning."

"Tessa, we heard how brave you have been and wanted to meet you," I said, "and our children send their greetings."

The nursing staff brought in more chairs, and we visited through lunch and into the afternoon. At about four o'clock, Michael went over to Tessa's bedside, leaned down, and whispered to her, "Would it be all right with you if we took your daddy to dinner with us? I promise to have him back here early."

Tessa nodded her head in agreement.

As we said our good-byes, I said to her, "Tessa, my family and I will be going home to Fiddyment. But I want you to know that you are in our prayers, and we'll be back soon for a visit. Okay?"

As we drove to Lake Forest, the conversation was light, but Armando remained quiet. A tear trickled out of his eye and slowly made its way down his cheek. He wiped it with the back of his hand.

I looked at him and smiled.

Armando smiled back and said, "I am blessed with friends."

When we entered the house, wonderful aromas wafted through to greet us.

"Oh my goodness. It smells absolutely great in here!" I exclaimed. "What can I do to help?"

"Make a huge tossed salad," Gail yelled from the kitchen. "Everything you'll need is in the fridge. Pearl and I have everything else under control. We're having a feast tonight!"

"Papa Jeff, Papa Jeff!" Jameson yelled as he entered the kitchen and beelined for Jeff.

"What's that?" Jeff countered as he picked up Jameson and put him on his back with his little legs dangling over his shoulders.

"Well," Jameson began, "today I told Aunt Pearl that she should be my gammy, and she said yes, she should. And you have the same white hair as her." He pulled Jeff's white locks back from his forehead. "So, you should be my papa." It all seemed very simple to Jameson.

"Well, young man, are you inferring that I'm old?" Jeff asked.

"Huh?" Jameson said. "What's infer…?"

"Inferring means, well…it means—oh, never mind. Yes, you may call me Papa Jeff. I would consider it an honor," Jeff stated.

Jeff looked at Pearl. "Well, Lady Pearl, it looks like we have become grandparents! Tell me…how many grandchildren do we have?"

"Four. Abby, Gabby, Cathy with a C, and Jameson. I'll give you a list of their birthdays later," Pearl told him and winked.

"Okay, everyone, please find your place at the table. We're ready to eat!" Gail announced.

At first, Armando was quiet and reserved. It didn't take long for him to join in the revelry of the group, tease the children, and tell a story or two. We liked him immediately. Jeff reminded Armando about the little boy who had been carried off by the tornado. We could see a gold tooth when he smiled and recalled the story.

"Ah, that was *you,* little one?" he said in his Spanish accent. "I can't imagine being carried away by the wind except while riding a horse!"

"That reminds me, Armando," Jeff said. "I told Jameson that you might be willing to take him for a ride when they come down to the farm."

"Oh, *si, si,* Señor. I would be happy to *titch* him," Armando agreed.

"*Titch* him?" I asked.

"C'mon, Lucy," Jeff chided. "Put on your Spanish ears!"

"Titch. Hmmmm...Oh! Teach!" I said.

Michael stood and said to Armando, "I promised Tessa we'd get you back early, so we should leave pretty soon. Aunt Pearl, care to go along for the ride?"

"Yes, I would," she answered.

Armando went around to each member of the group and expressed his gratitude for the hospitality and interest in his granddaughter. Tears brimmed in his eyes.

"Persnick," Tom said, "we'll stay the night and leave in the morning after breakfast, okay?"

"Oh, Tom—I'm sorry I didn't let you know sooner, but I just this instant decided. I'm going to be staying here for a day or two longer," she answered. "I've got some business to attend to."

Chapter 12

The three men and Pearl entered the hospital room, and Pearl went immediately to Tessa's bedside.

"Hello, Tessa. I'm Michael's Aunt Pearl, and I came along for the ride to bring your grandpapa back to you. And of course to meet you!"

Pearl looked for an unburned place on Tessa's small frame that she could touch or stroke, and found none.

"Jefferson told us about your accident and I am so sorry you have had such a horrible experience, but I want you to know that I believe everything will turn out just fine. It might take many surgeries and more time than you want, but it's *your* job to hold onto that. You *will* be fine. You are precious to us and we are here for you. Don't build walls of protection around yourself. Remember this, Tessa—the walls we build to keep out sadness, also keep out joy. Don't lose your joy. God bless you, child."

Tessa nodded her head and smiled.

Armando and the other men had moved over to the bedside.

"Ah, little one," Armando said, "we are very blessed to have such friends."

A nurse came in to change the IV solution, and she told the group that Tessa had a good evening and her surgery was scheduled for seven a.m.

"Señor Vasquez, we have a bed made for you on the other side of the room so you can spend the night," the nurse said.

"Oh, *muchas gracias, Señora,*" Armando said. "I do appreciate it."

The nurse looked at us and whispered, "Visiting hours are over in ten minutes."

"Oh, okay. Thank you for letting us know," Jefferson said.

"Armando, is there anything you need before we go?" Jefferson asked.

"No, Señor," Armando answered. "After Tessa is asleep, I will join the other overnight guests in the TV lounge for a while. We have all formed a little support group."

"Okay then. We'll be off, but I'll be back in the morning," Jefferson told him.

In the car, Pearl said, "I think it was good to bring him home with you this afternoon. Gave him a change of pace. But I'm so glad I met Tessa this evening. What a sweet child."

Chapter 13

The next morning, Tom and I brought our luggage to the main house so that we could leave right after breakfast. Jeff had borrowed one of Michael's cars and left early for the hospital to go be with Armando. All four kids were sitting quietly at the counter having breakfast. Abby and Gabby had packed for Cathy and Jameson, and their luggage was sitting off in a corner. Taffy could tell there was going to be a change, and she pranced around the kitchen going from person to person, nudging each.

"Mama!" Jameson exclaimed when he saw me. "Do we really have to go home? Really?"

"Yes, of course we must go home, but I'm sure we'll be invited back," I said.

"Yes, you will. You have an open invitation," Michael said to Jameson while he ruffled his hair.

"What does that mean?" Jameson asked.

"Open invitation means you can come back here—and I'm assuming we can come to you—any time it is convenient for both of us," Michael said.

"Naturally," I answered. "We have become like family it seems to me. And I love it."

As Gail and I cleared the table, the phone rang. Michael answered.

"Oh, that's good news...Uh-huh. Uh-huh...Yes. I see. Okay. Thank you for letting us know, Jeff," he said. Then he turned to us.

"This is what I know. The surgery is over and she's in recovery. So far, everything has gone like clockwork. Her hands had the most damage, but the areas that weren't burned are healthy and blood is flowing. It doesn't sound like they'll have to amputate. Not even her fingers. They grafted skin onto her arms, hands, and fingers so she'll be in a sterile environment for a few days. And Armando sends his greetings and thanks. I told Jeff this morning that I would take care of any plastic or reconstructive surgery she may need."

All of us let out a sigh of relief. I briefly explained to Jameson and Cathy what *amputate* meant. They were old enough to know that some people had difficult experiences. Life wasn't always cotton candy.

"Well, we should get going, Lucy," Tom said. "Kids, can you get your suitcases and take them to the car?"

"Yes, Daddy," said Cathy.

It was hard for Cathy and Jameson to say good-bye to Pearl, even though her visit had been extended for only a couple of days. They had really grown attached to her.

"Oh, kiddles," she laughed as she embraced them, "I'll be back in Fiddyment before you know it! You must be sure to tell Chester that I'll be home soon. And be sure to thank Penelope for looking out for him."

And you wouldn't believe the tears that spilled when they said good-bye to Abby and Gabby.

"Will you come see us soon?" Jameson sniffed.

"Sure will," the twins answered in unison.

After we left, Pearl said to Michael, "Can you go with me to the attorney's office this morning? There's something I want to do."

"Yes, of course. I'll call and tell him we're coming," Michael said as he picked up the phone.

"Good morning, Helen. Aunt Pearl and I will be stopping over to see Ed this morning, so give him a heads-up for us please. No, sorry. I don't know what she has in mind," he said.

Chapter 14

"Michael, you wait here," Pearl instructed Michael. She entered Ed's office. It was large and comfortable. Ed sat behind a massive desk with client files stacked neatly to one side; he stood and rounded the desk's corner to greet Pearl. He looked like he was ready for court. He was about Pearl's age, dressed in a dark blue suit, a crisply starched white shirt, and a pale blue tie.

"Why, Pearl Witsche. It's been a long time since I've had the pleasure of a visit from you. What is on your mind today?" he asked politely as he sat across from her.

Pearl leaned forward and explained what she wanted and how she had come to this decision. When she finished, she sat back in her chair and waited for his response.

He drummed the desktop with his pencil and looked her in the eye.

"Of course I will draw up the papers for you. It will be a delightful diversion from my normal routine. Good for you! Do you have a date in mind?"

"I sure do. Christmas!"

Chapter 15

Our phone was ringing as we entered the front door. It was the man Tom had contacted to do the repairs on the back of our house.

"Yeah, sure thing. C'mon over. Thirty minutes? Great! We'll put the coffee on," Tom said.

Exactly thirty minutes later, we heard the old truck's engine grind to a stop with a wheeze and a hiccup. Tom met him outside and they went around to the backyard. If his promptness was any indication, Hank Bloomberg would be as good as his word.

Hank was originally from Maine and had a thick New England accent. He was short, squatty, had holes in his T-shirt (which advertised his handyman business), a receding hairline, and the remainder of his hair was wild and unruly. He wore a baseball cap to protect his balding head from the sun, and he kept a pencil behind his ear.

"*Ayuh*, the tornado did some pretty good damage, she did," Hank said as he walked around examining the porch and house. "Ayuh, it should take a week to ten days to get 'er all fixed up."

"Okay," Tom said. "*Ayuh.* Exactly what is that?" Tom asked.

"Ayuh is ayuh," Hank answered.

"But what *is* ayuh?" Tom persisted.

"Ayuh is *yes* or *yeah,*" Hank said when he tried to remove his accent.

"Oh, I see. A week to ten days. That sounds pretty reasonable. When can you start?" Tom asked.

"Tomarra, seven o'clock," Hank replied with that New England lilt to his voice.

"Tomorrow. Good," Tom said as they shook hands.

Chester was very happy to see us and rubbed against my legs as I began preparations for lunch. He mewed and purred and went from me to Cathy to Jameson and then stood back and looked up at all of us as if to say, "Well? Where's Pearl?"

Jameson sat on the floor and pulled Chester onto his lap. He stroked his head and whispered, "Gammy Pearl will be back in a couple of days, Chester."

Our weekend respite at the Morgan's home had been just what we needed. Before that, I had been overwhelmed with tackling the clean-up which the tornado had so forcefully given me. And now to have the repairs underway would be good. When Tom came in, he told me that Hank had recommended someone to put in the pool.

"And I'll give him a call this afternoon when I get back from Three M. Do you know what shape you would like the pool to be?" Tom asked me.

"Gee, I don't know," I answered. "I'd just thought rectangle or kidney-shaped. Maybe he's got pictures of other pools he's done."

"Good idea. I'll ask him when I talk to him," Tom said as he poured a cup of coffee.

That afternoon, Tom came home flushed and sweaty. It was mid-August and very hot. Tom took the stairs two at a time to go up and take a shower and came down looking refreshed. I handed him a glass of iced tea, and he pulled out a slip of paper and sat beside the phone.

"Wonder if this guy can work a miracle and give me a pool today?" Tom muttered to himself as he dialed. "Yes, hello, is this Smitty Johnson? This is Tom Maguire and I got your name from Hank Bloomberg. Yes, that's right. He's going to repair some tornado damage to our house, and my wife and I are interested in putting in a pool in the backyard."

After several seconds, he said, "Sounds good. Well, Hank is starting in the morning, but I can show you the backyard. Do you have pictures of other pools you could show us? Great! How is ten o'clock? Great. See you then."

At seven a.m. sharp the next morning, we heard activity in the backyard. Hank and his crew were setting up saw horses, wood, ladders, and all the supplies they would possibly need to repair the back porch and damaged sections of the house. As soon as Jameson heard all the noise, he was up and out the door.

"Jus' hold it right there, Mistah," Hank said to Jameson as he walked over to Jameson, bent down, and looked him in the eye. "Are you planning to cause me trouble?"

"N-n-n-no, sir," Jameson stuttered. Poor little guy looked scared to death.

"Good. It's fine with me if you watch, but my rules are you can't touch anything, you can't get in the way, you can't ask questions, and you can't talk to my crew. The second you break just one of my rules, you're out of here. Got it?"

"Yes, sir," Jameson answered timidly.

"And if you *are* out here, you have to wear close-toed shoes—not those silly flip-flop things that go between your toes. We try to be careful, but sometimes we drop a nail. Okay?" Hank continued.

I stood on the porch, listening, and nodded my head in agreement. Then I introduced myself.

"Hank, I'm Lucy. Would you like some coffee?" I asked.

"Ayuh," he said and turned toward his truck. "Brought my own, thank you," and he held up a thermos.

"Oh. All right then," I said and went back into the kitchen.

Hank came up to the porch with a tape measure and pad, took the pencil from behind his ear, removed the plyboard Tom had put over the window, and looked closely at the gaping hole in the window. He whistled when he looked through the window into the kitchen. Jameson had put on sneakers, and like a shadow, followed him around the porch.

"Good thing you weren't standing here when the tree limb came through," he said to me as he measured.

"Not a chance," I said. "I was hiding in the cedar closet. Others were in the storm cellar. Jameson got picked up by the tornado."

"Was that him?" Hank asked. "Ayuh, I saw him on television. He's a brave boy. And you're a brave mama. What's his name again?"

"Jameson," I replied.

"Jameson," Hank said to himself. "That suits him. You interested in having a winda box? You know...a bump-out from the kitchen?"

"No," I answered, "but a pass-through would be nice."

"Ayuh, t'would," he said. "All right. I'll be going to the hardware store for a new winda, and I'll be back before you can say 'li'l Jameson Maguire ate a toasted peanut butter and grape jelly sandwich with sliced bananas and diced dill pickles.'" He winked at Jameson and went down the stairs. While I was trying to imagine what that would taste like, the old truck backed out of the driveway. I shivered and made a sourpuss face.

"Mama, can I have that for lunch? Where'd that man go?" Jameson asked.

"He went to get us a new kitchen window," I answered.

"Well, sometimes I don't know what he's saying. I thought he said 'winda,'" Jameson said. "Is a winda a window?"

"Jameson, Hank has a very thick New England accent, which means he pronounces things a little differently than we do. There are different accents all over the United States. Some people would say that we have a 'Midwest' accent," I explained.

"I don't have an accent," Jameson protested.

"Not to *our* ears, Jameson, but to others we might sound very strange. As you grow up and travel around a little bit, you'll begin to notice the differences," I continued.

"Oh. Okay. Mama, when will Gammy Pearl come back?" he asked.

"I think today or tomorrow," I said. "Do you miss her?"

"Yes. And so does Chester," Jameson said.

A little while later, Hank returned and before I knew it the new window had been installed. Then I heard the doorbell and the door open.

"Hey. You must be Smitty," Tom said.

"Yes, sir, I am," Smitty said as he pumped Tom's hand up and down.

"Well, come on in here and let's see what you've got," Tom said. "Would you like a cup of coffee?" Tom asked as he led him into the kitchen.

Smitty spotted Hank working outside and yelled his name.

"Hank! You doing a good job for these people?"

"Ayuh. You betcha. And I 'spect you to do the same!" Hank yelled back.

"I always do. I learned from the best!" Smitty hollered.

Smitty plunked a photo album down on the table and took the cup of coffee I was holding.

"Let me just have a peek at the backyard," he said as he walked out the back door and down the stairs.

When he came back in, he stopped at the coffeepot and looked at me.

"Oh, help yourself," I said and watched him pour more coffee into the cup.

"You folks like to join me at the table?" he asked Tom and me. "Tell me what you have in mind," he said as he opened the album.

"A *cee-ment* pond," Tom said as he mimicked the Beverly Hillbillies and winked at me.

"A deep end and a shallow end," I said. "And a slope going into the deep end."

"A diving board. And a Jacuzzi," Tom said.

"And a cabana," I said. "And an area to sunbathe."

"Did you want the entire yard cemented?" Smitty asked.

"Heavens no!" I exclaimed. "I've got a green thumb and like to play in the dirt, and the kids will want another swingset. The tornado got the other one," I offered.

"Okay," Smitty said as he turned the page of the album. "Let's see if you like any of these."

About an hour later, we came to an agreement and liked the backyard plans that Smitty had drawn for us as we talked. He told us that he could start when Hank was finished.

Smitty stood and went to the back door.

"Hey, Hank! When are you likely to finish up this job?" Smitty asked.

"Oh, about a week, I think. Go faster if you'd help," Hank replied in his thick Maine accent.

"Okay, it's a deal," Smitty said. He turned toward us.

"I'll go out and give them a hand. I used to work for Hank before I struck out on my own, and I can keep the crew motivated. Thanks for the coffee!" he said and the screen door slammed shut behind him.

The next time I saw Smitty, he was wearing a tool belt and was climbing a ladder.

As I expected, Pearl returned the next day and Jeff had come along for the ride with the understanding that Michael would take him to O'Hare Airport on the return trip. Tessa was doing well, and the skin graft was "holding." They explained much of that to us over lunch, and I had a good time watching the exchange between Pearl and Jeff. I had never seen a spark like this in Pearl's eye and at one point I looked at Michael over the table and raised my eyebrows. All he could do was shrug. Without a conversation with Michael, I knew we were in "wait and see" mode.

The work crew was making good progress on the back side of our house, and the three men went outside to inspect the work. Smitty came over and described where the pool would go and some of the other features we had chosen.

As Michael and Jeff prepared to leave, I seized the opportunity to talk about the approaching holidays.

"Hey, everyone. I rather like this family and extended family and I'd like to invite the Morgans, Jeff, and of course, Pearl, to have Thanksgiving here with us. Between Pearl's home and ours, there's room for everybody, and I know we'd have a good time. How about it?"

Michael spoke first.

"Gail and I have been talking about the holidays too, and I think Thanksgiving would be great here if you'll all come to our place for Christmas!" he said.

Jeff was the first to respond.

"I'd like that," said Jeff, "so count me in. In fact, I'll be back before then, and I'm serious about going to a Fiddyment football game! I can *rah! rah! rah!* just as good as everyone else!"

"Oh," said Tom, "I picked up a home game schedule... now where did I put it..." Tom said, scratching his head as he went on a search.

"Check your pockets," I yelled after him. "I haven't done the laundry yet."

Tom returned with a crumpled piece of paper.

"Here you go, Jeff. Sorry about...guess I was in a hurry," Tom said sheepishly as he unfolded the paper.

"Great. Thanks. Now I'll know how to schedule trips," Jeff replied.

"We'd better get going, Jeff. You've got a plane to catch," Michael said.

Jefferson said good-bye, hugging each of us. Then he got to Pearl. At first, they shook hands, then Jefferson pulled her into his arms for an embrace. I watched her smile and blush. I wanted to tease her, but decided against it. Both Cathy and Jameson hugged Papa Jeff tightly and had great big tears in their eyes.

We stood and waved as the car backed out of the driveway and sped off down the street.

Chapter 16

Things happened fast. The house repairs were completed and now the pool was underway. There was an enormous hole in the backyard, and I was curious about what would happen next. We all hoped it would be ready for a swim or two before Labor Day. Smitty had promised to give us lessons on the care and management of pool ownership and would teach us how to check the chemicals. Pearl was barely limping these days and felt well enough to live on her own again, so she and Chester returned to her cottage. The kids and I missed her like crazy, but before long, it was Maguire routine as usual. Now we had the added feature of Pearl riding her bike over to give Cathy a dulcimer lesson. Cathy loved it, learned fast, and she was quite good. Pearl said she was a natural.

Pearl went with me to look at the general store one afternoon. It had character, history, and lots of dust. If only the walls could talk! We walked every inch of the store while Pearl reminisced about things that had happened, conversations, and interesting Fiddyment shoppers. I thought it might be fun to resurrect the concept of having a general store; Pearl made several suggestions, including antiques, a coffee or tea shop, candy store, craft shop, a section for children's books, classes on quilt making, or even teaching dulcimer. Once the windows were cleaned, there would be good light coming in the front and back windows. It could be fun, charming, and whimsical. Now my head was spinning with ideas. Whatever was decided, it needed a good, catchy name. I still wanted to go around to Fiddyment's store owners and talk about beautifying their store fronts. Suddenly, I had an idea.

"Pearl," I began, "could we get this place straightened up enough to have a meeting here? Maybe have a few plants here as gifts for the Fiddyment shops, and serve dessert and coffee? I could even make invitations and deliver them."

"Why yes, I think we could," Pearl said. "Let's go over to the greenhouse to see how many plants we have there. And I'll check my own garden." She had instantly captured my vision and enthusiasm.

We had been in constant communication with the Morgans and had learned that Armando had returned to Easterbrook Farm for a while and it just about broke his heart to leave Tessa. Gail had promised him that she would look in on Tessa and even take her on outings. Tessa had progressed nicely and was now waiting for yet another skin graft. The only thing was that Tessa was depressed, didn't want people to see her, and was withdrawn.

I was reaching for the phone to make a call when it rang; I was so startled I just about jumped out of my skin.

"Hi, Lucy, it's Gail. Would you be interested in having guests on Saturday? We're 'springing' Tessa from the hospital and thought we'd take a ride in your direction," she said.

"Absolutely!" I said. "My kids have heard quite a bit about Tessa and would love to meet her. There's one teensy problem. Pearl and I are planning to clean the old general store this week for a meeting with the town's business owners, and we need to do the finishing touches on Saturday. When do you think you'd get here?"

"Not sure. But we'd be happy to give you a hand. How about if we stop by your place and if you're not there, we'll just head over to the store? I bet Michael would like to take a walk down memory lane anyway."

And so, the very next day, Pearl and I arrived at the general store with buckets, brooms, mops, rags, cleaning supplies, and ideas. A radio played in the background while we swept, mopped, dusted, polished, and packed. Throughout the week, we arranged the old counters, the old barber chair, found an old braided rug and placed it, and brought in borrowed chairs from the church, and plants, plants, and more plants. We had candles and several lamps in various locations so there would be soft lighting. Then we began to bake.

Chapter 17

Pearl arrived early Saturday morning with a huge coffee urn in her bicycle basket for us to take over to the general store. I heard her knock the kickstand down with her foot and climb the back stairs. I was taking a pan of oatmeal chocolate chip cookies out of the oven when she came in through the back door. Peanut butter cookies were on the counter waiting to be packed.

"Hi, all! The pool will be done before you know it," Pearl said as she glanced at the backyard. "You could probably have a summer's end pool party if you wanted."

"Yes, I bet we could," I replied. "But I'll have to think about that tomorrow."

"Right. What can I do?" Pearl asked as she poured a cup of tea.

"Uh, I think we're just about there," I answered. "Pearl, maybe you could get things out of the freezer and put them in these boxes."

"Sure," she replied and opened the freezer door. "Wow! You've really been busy."

"Well, I didn't want to run out. Ready? Let's go!"

As we finished last minute preparations for the meeting that afternoon, I wandered around the counters and let my fingers drift over the old wood. We had polished everything to a brilliant sheen. As I looked toward the ceiling,

I could almost hear voices from the past. I still needed to decide what I wanted to do with this charming old building. The sound of voices brought me back from my delightful daydream. It was the Morgans and Tessa.

"Hello!" I yelled from the back of the room. I think I must have sounded like an owl. "What do you think?"

"Wow!" Michael said. "The windows are clean! It really looks different with this kind of furniture in here!"

"I know, right? The windows have been my job," Tom said from behind a counter.

"Gail?" I asked.

"I think it's perfect for today," she replied. "When you know what you are going to do in here, I'll help you with it all. Okay?" She grabbed a vase and cut flowers and began to arrange them.

"Oh, I was hoping you'd say that!" I said.

Michael handed me a sign he had carved.

"What's this?" I asked.

"Gail told me the name you were thinking about. If you've changed your mind, I'll make another," Michael said.

"Pearl's Gate," I read. "Well, I have changed my mind, but I want to have a children's reading corner…probably in the back…and call it "Pearl's Gate"…and have it look similar to the front yard and porch of Pearl's cottage surrounded by a little white picket fence to set it apart. I absolutely love the sign, Michael. Thank you." I touched my cheek to his.

Cathy and Jameson didn't wait to be introduced to Tessa. They warmly accepted her into the family. Unafraid, Jameson chattered away and asked her questions about the accident and the various surgeries.

"I'm glad you're feelin' better," Jameson said to Tessa. "You'll be all better soon. Don't worry about it." He patted her bandaged hand. Tessa felt comfortable with the children and actually smiled.

"Lucy Maguire? Is there a Lucy Maguire here?" a voice from the doorway said.

"Yes. Over here!" I yelled.

"I have a delivery for you," the voice replied.

He came in carrying a huge balloon bouquet and handed me an envelope.

When I opened the envelope, it read:

> Dear Lucy,
>
> I know you and Pearl will have an abundance of flowers around to beautify the store and make a point to the community. But sometimes you need something that puts a smile on your face. Know that I am thinking of you and will see you soon. How's a week? Get my room ready!
>
> Armando will be coming with me!
>
> Best regards,
> Jefferson Easterbrook

Jameson's hands flew to his chubby cheeks. Cathy jumped up and down. Pearl smiled and blushed.

"Papa Jeff is coming! Papa Jeff is coming!" Jameson chirped over and over.

"And my grandpa," Tessa quietly reminded them.

"It will be good to see both of them," I said. "Now, Pearl, let's get this event ready!"

Michael, Gail, and Tom took the children home so Pearl and I could give our full attention to the presentation. We heard a tinkling bell as the first guest arrived, and the second, and the next. Before we knew it, the general store was full of Fiddyment store owners and merchants.

We showed pictures and signage of other small towns, such as Lake Forest, Wheaton, and Long Grove, and demonstrated different ways to make customers feel welcomed. We encouraged questions and conversation. We asked for their ideas. We began to sense that they were excited. We served dessert, we gave away plants with watering instructions, and took orders for more plants. All in all, the event was a success. Now it was up to them to get the Village of Fiddyment on the map.

Meeting with the townspeople was exhilarating for me, but at the same time, I was anxious to get home and visit with the Morgans. When Pearl and I walked in the door, Michael was telling Tessa that he was going to perform plastic surgery on her at the right time and he explained more about it.

"Michael?" I said. "I knew you were a physician, but I didn't know that you are a plastic surgeon! How appropriate for you to use your hands and fingers like that!"

"You didn't know? I guess it never came up. Yeah, my ability to see beauty in a piece of wood and whittling it to reality came in handy after all," he humbly replied.

By Monday afternoon, we were aware that our suggestions to spruce up the stores and shops inside and out had been effective. The hardware store sold paint and brushes. Merchants washed their storefront windows and displayed their wares and made their particular shop inviting so that passersby would be drawn in. Brochures were distributed. Sales were advertised. Pots of flowers were placed to one side of the doorways or hung on outdoor plant hooks. Park benches were placed along the sidewalk. Wonderful aromas of baked bread and chocolate were carried on the breeze from the bakery. Plates of pies, cakes, and cookies were placed in the window to entice shoppers. Scooper

Dooper offered free tastes of ice cream. An ice cream table and accompanying chairs were placed out front. The dress shop had a sidewalk sale. Even the gas station had big pots of flowers and coffee brewing for its customers. Fiddyment always had the basics, but now the facelift was successful. Now it was becoming charming.

Our swimming pool was finished and filled with water that glistened in the sun. The children splashed and swam while I sat in a lounge chair and read, or visited with Pearl or Penelope. And then Jeff arrived.

Chapter 18

Throughout the fall, Jefferson stayed with us whenever he visited. He and Tom worked together on household projects; they closed the pool at the end of September. A couple of weeks later, the weather turned and the seasons changed. Jefferson went with us to football games and cheered right along with the folks from Fiddyment. He even worked at the refreshment stand. He and Pearl went for bike rides and picnics. One Saturday, Tom and Jeff went over to Pearl's and worked on her car. It just needed a few adjustments, and then it sputtered to a start. Jeff was charming, dapper, suave, a perfectly fine Southern gentleman. He was smitten with Pearl and wasn't ashamed to show it. During the times he spent with us, I watched Pearl watching him. She had known of this man for years; she had even been attracted to him as a young woman. But Willowby had won her over while Jeff was actively getting into the horse-racing business.

One day Pearl and I were alone in the house. Tom and Jeff had taken the kiddles to visit Tessa after another surgery and were due home around suppertime. I seized the opportunity to talk to Pearl.

"So, Pearl…" I began as I rolled out pie dough, "what do you think about Jefferson? Seems to me—"

"Oh, dear," she interrupted, almost giddily, "I don't know what to think! He's wonderful…kind…gentle…and my knees go weak when he looks at me. Or when I look at him! I feel like a schoolgirl again."

"Nothing wrong with that, Pearl," I said. "What would you tell me if the shoe were on the other foot?"

"I'd tell you to relax and let it happen."

"Good. Then take your own advice."

Tom, Jeff, and the kids returned, and we were just about ready to sit down to dinner when Jeff began to tell us about their visit at the hospital. Michael had told Tessa that she would be released soon—she could return to Easterbrook Farm and have follow-up appointments with a doctor that Michael recommended.

"So I'd like to suggest a slight change of plans…that all of you and Michael's family come to Easterbrook Farm for Thanksgiving. What do you think about that, Jameson? You could ride the wind on one of Armando's favorite horses like I promised you!"

We looked at each other and in unison we all said, "*Yes!*"

Chapter 19

Anticipating a great long weekend in Kentucky, we packed the car, picked up Pearl at her cottage, and headed south early on the Wednesday morning before Thanksgiving. During the trip, we sang songs, told stories, and played games as the miles ticked by. We ate bologna sandwiches and cookies. The kids watched for Burma Shave markers and the accompanying jingles. We all liked, *"Cattle crossing means go slow. That old bull is some cow's beau. Burma Shave"* and *"Slow down, Pa; sakes alive; Ma missed signs four and five. Burma Shave."* The blue sky was filled with fluffy clouds; telephone poles and leafless trees were a blur in the car windows as we drove south through rolling hills and unfamiliar landscapes. Early in the afternoon outside of Lexington, we spotted the sign for Easterbrook Farm and turned onto the long tree-lined driveway. There were fenced-in pastures on both sides of the drive, the corral, and then the driveway opened onto a clearing. Before us was the main house—the bunkhouse—and stables were off to the side. Abby, Gabby, and Tessa spied us coming and everyone was waiting outside. The kiddles opened the car doors and everybody talked at the same time. It felt good to see them. It felt good to be at the farm.

Almost the second Jameson emerged from the car, he asked to see the horses. Armando grabbed Cathy's and Jameson's hands and took them to the stable.

"First, *leetle* ones, you must put on the saddle before you ride."

We had all been around Armando long enough, that we easily understood his accent.

"But I'm not big enough," Jameson protested.

Several minutes later, all five kids were riding. Cathy rode with Abby; Jameson rode with Armando. At first Jameson looked frightened, but he relaxed and his lips formed a huge grin. Armando took the horse to a fast gait and eventually handed the reins to Jameson, who loved riding this huge horse, and he made Armando promise that they would ride again before they went home.

"When you are older and can ride alone, you'll be able to ride like the wind, Tweester," Armando told Jameson.

While the horses were brushed and returned to the stable, I glanced toward Pearl. Her eyes sparkled, and there was a faint blush on her cheeks. She put her arm through the crook of Jeff's and they walked toward the main house. The Morgans and Tessa had arrived the day before and had purchased the turkey and other supplies to make the side dishes, and Gail had already made two pies—pumpkin and chocolate pecan. She had even done a little Thanksgiving decorating with gourds, Indian corn, and candles, so the home was festive and ready to receive guests. Gail quietly placed a meatloaf and foil-wrapped potatoes in the oven for our meal together. That evening, light chatter became a party atmosphere. We played a couple of board games. Jefferson put a stack of 33s on the record player and moved toward Pearl.

"May I have this dance, Lady Pearl?"

I watched her walk into his open arms, and I knew at that moment that his intentions with her were gallant and noble. Soon we were all dancing to the tunes of Andy Williams, the Beatles, Elvis, the Mamas and Papas, and Johnny Mathis as the vinyl records spun around and around on the record player.

That night as Tom and I snuggled in bed, I whispered to him, "I bet he'll propose one of these days." Tom muttered some kind of response and then snored as he fell asleep.

It was incredible to me to notice how comfortable we all were with each other in this extended family. The women all worked well together in the kitchen and put together a fabulous Thanksgiving feast. Armando and Tessa joined us for Thanksgiving dinner. Each person was asked to say one thing they were thankful for. Jameson was thankful that he got to ride Night Dancer; Tessa said that she was grateful for Dr. Michael; Armando said that he was thankful to finally have his beautiful granddaughter home. She beamed with the compliment.

I held my breath and touched Tom's knee, waiting for Jeff to speak. He cleared his throat a couple of times and then said, "I'm thankful for all of you, that you consider me part of your family, and that you drove all the way here for Thanksgiving. I'm thankful that Pearl is in my life...and I hope she's glad to have me in hers."

He stopped. He waited. He finally glanced at her. A tear slid down her cheek, and she nodded her head up and down as she agreed.

"Hallelujah!" he whispered to himself. "Let's be seated and thank the Good Lord for his blessings, and enjoy this bounty. It sure smells good."

After dinner, we settled in the living room in front of the roaring stone fireplace. A white bearskin rug was stretched out in front of the crackling fire. Cathy sat on it and rubbed the fur. Michael rearranged the burning logs and stirred the embers. Jeff's home was a sprawling farmhouse made of logs. Wood beams extended across the ceiling; it was nicely decorated with leather furniture and animal hides, but lacked a woman's touch. The kids sat at a game table and worked on an interesting, but difficult, jigsaw puzzle of a winter scene.

I placed my coffee mug on the side table. I looked around and whispered to Gail, "Where's Pearl?" She shrugged. I looked again. "And Jeff?" Another shrug, this time with raised eyebrows.

"So…Lucy," Gail began, "I think we should help Jefferson get this place ready for Christmas. Shall we go hunting for decorations? Think he has any?" she asked as she stood to her feet.

"I wish it would…" Cathy began to whine, but she was cut short.

Jeff and Pearl came in through the back door.

"It's snowing!" he announced. "C'mon outside!"

The kids scrambled to find their jackets and flew out the door. The air was filled with big, fluffy snowflakes that didn't take long to cover everything. The flakes landed softly on the ground and made a white, sparkling coverlet. Gabby gathered a handful of the fluff and tried to make a snowball, but all he could manage to throw were flakes that separated in the air. Jefferson laid himself on the ground and pulled Pearl down beside him; Jameson plopped himself beside Jeff and the three of them kicked their legs back and forth and put their arms overhead and then down to their sides. The rest of us joined them. An army of snow angels was about all that was going to happen since the snow wasn't wet and heavy enough to make snowballs or a snowman.

"Oh dear"—Pearl giggled quietly—"I haven't done that in a long, long time."

"Let's go get a tree in the morning!" Michael suggested. "Is there a tree nursery around here where we could cut our own tree?"

Jefferson told him that there was and that would be a fun outing for everybody; he even volunteered that there were decorations, garland, and lights in the attic. Then he and Pearl climbed the stairs to the porch; he stomped snow from his feet and winked at Pearl.

"Brrrr…it's cold out here. Let's go back inside where it's warm. We've got something to talk to you about," he remarked as he glanced toward Pearl.

The snow was tumbling from the sky and covered our coats and hair. The kids stuck out their tongues to catch snowflakes, but soon we were all gathered in front of the fireplace.

Jeff began, "I've just been showing Pearl around the stable because I wanted her to see the horses." He paused searching for the right words. "I've been thinking about giving up the thoroughbred horse business, which would involve a myriad of other decisions. And the accident investigation is still going on."

He took a quick glance toward his boots. Straw was on his right knee.

"Oh, I can explain this," he said as he wiped the straw from his knee. "You see," he continued, "I've talked to Pearl about a *couple* of things." He grabbed her hand.

The adults looked confused.

"The horses and…I've asked Pearl if she would marry me," he said excitedly. "And… she said yes!"

A huge smile filled her face. She extended her left arm and showed us the ring. It was a huge, round pearl surrounded by deep red rubies. It was gorgeous and absolutely perfect for Pearl. As well as congratulations, there was a flood of questions from all of us: When? Where would it take place? Why so soon? How could we help?

"You realize," Pearl calmly stated as Jameson climbed onto her lap and Cathy leaned against Jeff, "that this is all new news to everybody, but we will consider any suggestions and we'll talk about the plans this weekend and develop an outline for a small…" She paused. "Did you hear me? *Small* wedding. And don't you forget, Lucy," she continued with a wink in my direction, "that I am still persnickety. It will be simple, but lovely."

She giggled and rested her head on Jeff's shoulder. He kissed her forehead and whispered, "I love you, Lady Pearl."

Gail handed out small glasses of brandy. Michael raised his glass to make a toast.

"Best wishes to both of you. Aunt Pearl, I'm so happy for you and Jefferson. It's been a long time coming! Years, in fact! To Jefferson and Pearl!"

Jameson tugged on my sweater.

"Mama," he whispered loudly, trying to understand, "does that mean that Gammy won't be a witch anymore?"

Out of the mouths of babes.

Chapter 20

Life back at Fiddyment was very busy between Thanksgiving and Christmas. Tom had to give and grade science finals and conduct school and community concerts; the children were busy at school and getting restless for a winter break; I kept busy decorating for Christmas, shopping and wrapping gifts, and adding touches to the general store; Pearl made wedding plans and took me with her to shop for a dress (she wanted simple, but elegant). She and Jefferson had decided to get married on the Friday evening between Christmas and New Year's Day at the little church we attended. It made perfect sense since out-of-town guests would be able to come, the church would still be decorated with trees, poinsettias, and candles; the fellowship hall would be used for the cake and punch reception. And because of all the busyness, it was decided that Christmas for this ever-growing extended family would be at our house.

On Christmas Eve, we all attended the candlelight service at the church, which was exquisite with its décor of simply lit pine trees, poinsettias, green wreaths with huge plaid bows, and glowing candles; it gave us a prelude to the wedding in a few days. It was a charming service of Christmas carols, scriptures were read of shepherds, angels, the inn with no vacancies, and the birth of Jesus. At the end, Pearl played "Silent Night" on her hammered dulcimer. The evening was uncomplicated and flawless.

It snowed while we were inside the church. Enormous, heavy, snowflakes tumbled out of the sky and formed a blanket of shimmering white. By the time we placed cookies and milk beside the fireplace hearth for Santa, and tucked Cathy and Jameson into their beds, the snow had stacked up on roofs and bare branches and covered the earth like thick marshmallow fluff.

"Yes, of course Santa will be able to find our house. He loves the snow," Tom replied to Jameson's worried questions as he closed the bedroom door.

While Tom was upstairs, Pearl, Jefferson, and I started pulling gifts and toys from hidden places. Jefferson began to put together a train track around the tree. He stood and admired his work and then fidgeted with other things—a doll, a scooter, Play Doh, an Easy-Bake Oven, a slinky, Etch-A-Sketch, and a sled.

"I'm glad you decided to spend the night here," I commented to no one in particular. "The kids are so excited. They'll be up early to see what Santa brought. Pearl, I thought we could make cinnamon rolls in the morning. We'll have a nice breakfast before the Morgans arrive. Hope they don't have any trouble getting here."

"Yes, dear. I'm sure it was the best idea, especially in light of how heavy the snow is," Pearl replied. "And it will be wonderful to experience the joy of little ones in the morning, don't you agree, Jefferson?"

"Indeed, Lady Pearl. I've never had the opportunity, and as I know, neither have you," he answered as he sat beside her and placed his arm around her shoulders. "You can just feel their excitement." He stopped for a moment and rubbed his index finger along his mustache. "Pearl? I've been thinking, what would you think about staying up here for a while after our honeymoon? Maybe 'til spring? Armando will be fine with taking care of the horses at the farm. Besides, I'm only a phone call away."

"That sounds all right with me," Pearl said sleepily.

Chapter 21

Jameson threw back the covers and sat up. He rubbed his eyes. It was morning. It was Christmas morning. He didn't remember dreaming of sugar plums. Santa had come sometime during the night and Jameson hadn't even heard the sleigh bells or reindeer hooves on the roof or Santa calling out as he drove the sleigh full of toys through the sky.

He jumped to his feet and looked out the window. Deep, brilliant, white snow had piled and drifted into huge mounds. He flung open the door to his bedroom and tip-toed into the hallway. He rapped loudly on Jeff's door.

"Papa Jeff! Papa Jeff! Wake up! It's Christmas! C'mon downstairs, everybody! Wake up!"

As Jameson grabbed the banister at the top of the stairs, Jeff opened the door to the upstairs guestroom and stood there groggily.

"Are you sure Santa has been here, Jameson? It's kind of early." He tied his robe closed.

Jameson stared at him blankly as if to say, *So?*

Pearl had awakened earlier than Jameson and made coffee for the adults. She had circled the living room to make sure the bubble lights decorating the tree were bubbling, and she flipped the switch to the train so that it chugged around the tree. Finally, she placed a small package under the tree and pushed it with her toe.

"Gammy! You're up!" Then he saw the proof—the actual proof—that Santa had been there. "*Look!*" He pointed toward the tree.

Cathy was right behind him, squealing all the way down the stairs.

After toys from Santa had been examined and played with, gift boxes from the adults had been opened, and torn paper and ribbon pushed aside, Pearl exclaimed, "Oh my goodness! I think there's something else under the tree! Cathy? Can you reach it?"

Cathy carefully climbed over the train track, lay on her tummy under the fragrant, sticky boughs, and stretched her arm to get hold of the small package. Her arms weren't quite long enough, so she scooted closer to the wrapped gift. At last, it was within her grasp.

She looked at the tag as she scooted back out, went across the room, and handed it to her mother. "It's for you, Mama."

I looked around the room.

"Me?" I asked, puzzled.

I carefully removed the ribbon and gift wrap, and opened the lid. Inside was an envelope containing a beautifully penned, handwritten note. I read aloud:

> "My dear, Lucy~
>
> I consider it a gift of the heart—a treasure—that we have reconnected and bonded after so many years. As you know, your mother and I were best friends and so I knew you before you were born. I heard you speak your first words and I watched you

take your first steps. As your mother got sicker and sicker, she encouraged me to spend more and more time with you. And I did so gladly. I combed your hair and watched you play in Fiddyment Creek. We searched the sky for shapes and cloud animals. We made cupcakes. I did the things your mother could not. I watched her being ripped away from you by illness and I saw the abandonment of a disinterested father. I desperately wanted to adopt you—and even tried—but it wasn't to be. So I watched you grow up from afar and rode my bike past your home almost daily, hoping to get a glimpse of you. My heart beat so loudly and rapidly when we first spoke in front of the general store, I was sure you could hear it. Meeting the children that day was delightful. They are precious. I am so very proud of the woman, wife, and mother you have become.

Do you remember the weekend we spent at Michael's and I stayed behind while you came back home? I went to see my attorney. There is something called "adult adoption." I feel that we have become a family. This would make it legal. Will you allow me to adopt you? Even as an adult? Will you become my daughter whom I have loved forever? I would love to be your mother, and mother-in-law to Tom, and grandma to the children.

With undying love and affection,
Pearl

Tears spilled down my cheeks. The children were unable to understand exactly what was going on. Jameson climbed onto my lap, and Cathy asked, "Why you crying, Mama?"

"Because I'm overcome with happiness," I whispered. Our foreheads touched.

I looked toward the woman who had entered my life with her gentle ways and gentle spirit—the woman I had called Persnickety Witch.

"Yes, Pearl. *Yes!*"

Chapter 22

The Morgans had to shovel their driveway before they could begin their exciting, but exhausting, drive to Fiddyment. The roads hadn't been plowed, and Michael followed the tracks left by previous drivers. Two hours later, they arrived at our home.

After Christmas dinner, the kids all went outside to build snowmen and have a snowball fight. They took the new sled out and pulled each other. The men sat at the dining room table and played cards. Pearl asked Gail if she would like to see her dress.

"Oh my! Pearl, this dress is so…so…*you!* It's simple but elegant. You'll look absolutely stunning!" Gail exclaimed. "Has Jeff seen it yet?"

"Of course not!" Pearl whispered excitedly.

My heart smiled. This woman would soon be my mother.

I heard loud guffaws and my attention was drawn to the window. Even though the kids were having lots of fun playing in the snow, I knew they must be getting cold. I pulled mugs, cocoa powder, marshmallows from the cupboard, and milk from the refrigerator.

The back door opened and they came in, still laughing about who had built the best snowman. They had stomped and removed their boots on the porch. Now the boots were lined up on a rug to catch the drips, and they hung their coats on hooks and rushed into the kitchen.

"So, if Pearl is going to be your mother," Abby began as she sipped the hot cocoa, "and she's already my aunt, what does that make us?" The question was directed to me.

"Ummm…cousins," I answered.

Cathy's head raised. "Cousins? Cool. Jameson, we have cousins."

Chapter 23

Each pew of the small church was occupied with wedding guests from all over the United States. A light conversational buzz filled the room. The exquisite stained-glass windows glimmered with the reflection of candles. Poinsettias lined the center aisle and the platform. In the back and front of the church, several Christmas trees were decorated with strings of white lights. It was enchanting. The church organist played several familiar melodies. The back door creaked and opened. The crowd turned.

There they were, looking exactly like royalty. Pearl and Jefferson stood side by side with an aura of happiness surrounding them. Jefferson was extremely handsome with his thick, wavy white hair and dark eyes. He was dressed in a three-piece black suit, starched white shirt, and black tie. Pearl was radiant. A single strand of pearls circled her neck and small pearl cluster earrings had been fastened to her ears. Her hair was in a lovely chignon at the nape of her neck. Today there were no wisps escaping from beneath a straw hat. She wore a floor-length, long-sleeved, winter white, velvet A-line dress. White fur was on the scooped neckline. She put her hands into a furry winter white muff. She was extraordinarily beautiful. She glowed, there was blushing color on her cheeks; her sapphire eyes sparkled.

"Ready?" Jefferson whispered to her.

She nodded once.

The music began and they walked together down the short aisle. The minister waited for them at the front of the church.

From the minister's welcoming comments to the vows to the final words, "You may kiss your bride," all these seemed to me like seconds and eons at the same time. My memories flew through my brain of my sick mother, meeting Tom, having my own babies, meeting Pearl, and all the things I had learned about my past and this glorious woman who was now my mother. I heard them say their vows. I wiped a tear that wanted to edge out of my eye. I watched Jeff tenderly kiss Pearl.

"It is my very distinct pleasure to introduce to you Mr. and Mrs. Jefferson Davis Easterbrook."

There was roaring applause. The organ began to play triumphantly. They again walked the aisle, this time arm in arm.

I just sat there and grinned until Tom squeezed my hand. "C'mon, Luce. It's time to join the receiving line."

We found our places beside the newlyweds in the lobby, and greeted the guests one by one until the sanctuary was empty. Downstairs, the fellowship hall was enchanting. The lighting was low, votive candles had been placed strategically around the room, chairs had been placed in semicircles for gathering and conversation, and a decorated tree stood in one corner. Tulle had been draped across the ceiling, offering a dreamlike appearance. A long table had been set up along the side. It held a crystal-footed punch bowl filled with a Christmas punch that Pearl had created, a three-tiered chocolate wedding cake (because chocolate was Jeff's favorite), small crystal bowls overflowed with mints and nuts, and crystal dessert plates and silverware at the ready.

Gail served punch; I cut the cake. Music was being played on a record player; someone had hung sprigs of mistletoe in all the doorways. Pearl and Jefferson moved easily from group to group, stopping briefly to chat. Pearl had been a resident of Fiddyment for a long time and she was well loved; Jefferson had been around enough during the courtship, so he had gotten to know many folks in the area.

"Well, everyone, this has been a wonderful and momentous occasion for us and we'd like to thank you for sharing it with us. How often do you get married at our ages? But right now, we've got a train to catch," Jeff announced to the crowd. "We'll see you when we return from our honeymoon!"

Chapter 24

The newlyweds were gone about a month, including stopping at Easterbrook Farm for a few days on their return. They had taken the train to a coastal city in Florida and boarded a ship for a Caribbean cruise. There was nothing like an island tour in the middle of winter; it was tropically hot, the skies were endless, clear, and bright blue. And so was the water. Often changing colors depending on clouds and the sun's position, the warm water was indigo, turquoise, azure, aqua, or jade-like green, but it was always crystal clear. They snorkeled off the shore of St. Croix, browsed through the tourist shops at the ports-o-call, purchased souvenirs, and sampled various local foods. They buried their toes in the sand, and they both tanned to a delicious shade of *café au lait*. Onboard, they danced, played shuffleboard, and dined with the other passengers. They spent many private moments deep in conversation about their future, Jeff's retirement, and the farm.

They lingered after dinner with another couple, Doug and Jen Miller, one evening toward the end of the cruise. The Millers were comfortable to be with, in their late thirties, curious about the thoroughbred horses, and interested in Easterbrook Farm.

"Well, one of the best features of the farm is my horse whisperer, Armando. But he told me before our wedding that he and his granddaughter are going to go back to Argentina so she has a chance to be with her family. That is, when she is finished with her treatment…which won't be long now. It's been really hard on her since her mama was killed in an accident."

"We wouldn't want to keep the race horses," the man said. "I'm a physician and Jen is a nurse, and I've been thinking about opening an equine therapy center. I believe people with special needs would benefit from therapy such as this. Your place sounds perfect."

Jefferson's head jerked up.

"Therapy? Did you say therapy?"

"Why, yes, I did."

"Tell me more," Jefferson suggested.

"Of course. First, let me say that Armando and Tessa could stay as long as they wanted. Maybe he would help me get things ready. Here's the nugget about horse therapy. Horses need a lot of care. When a patient is busy grooming, feeding, or exercising a horse, he isn't focusing on his own problems. This gives his mind a rest from the difficult issues he's facing. In addition, a patient has to learn new skills in order to care for a horse. Learning these skills increases self-confidence. Patients don't need to worry about rejection either, since horses are nonjudgmental.

"Horses are good animals to work with because they mirror the emotions of the people around them. If the person caring for it is aggressive, controlling, or noisy, the horse becomes fearful and responds negatively. Patients learn that their behavior affects others. In order to work with the horse, they have to learn how to change their behavior. Horses are herd animals. They need to feel safe and look for a leader to tell them what to do. A horse will cooperate with a person who makes requests instead of demands."

Pearl watched Jefferson and smiled. Jefferson looked her way.

"When do you want to see Easterbrook Farm?"

Chapter 25

With the sale of Easterbrook Farm underway, Tessa finishing treatment, Armando agreeing to stay on at the farm for a while, and Pearl and Jeff getting settled at the cottage, Pearl's attention could join mine on getting the general store ready to open. We created brochures and distributed them. We planned the opening. We came up with ideas to enhance it.

The old general store was bustling with activity as we prepared to remove butcher paper from the windows and unlock the door. People from far and wide had heard about this unique, happy place. There really was something for everybody. Brochures had been distributed at school. Newspaper ads beckoned everyone to come enjoy the experience. Children of all ages begged their parents to take them.

"Mama, Mama, I want to go there! When can we go? All the kids are talking about it."

A new sign made by Michael hung beside the front door, and another had been painted on the window. The front half of the building had been transformed into a unique coffee-and-tea shop. Decorated with antiques (including the cracker barrel and chess set), small tables and chairs were waiting for guests to enjoy their hot brew of choice and a sweet treat. The rear of the lower floor—the part that had originally been the barber's corner—had been transformed to be almost magical. That section had been designed as a porch with a swing and rocking chairs. A red Schwinn bicycle leaned against the fence. A resident cat, a very friendly Himalayan named Clover, had the run of the whole store, but more often than not, took her cat-naps on the swing. The area that might have been the yard was carpeted with green grass-like mats. The yard was surrounded by a white picket fence, and there was a sign hung on the creaky opening that said *Pearl's Gate.* Potted plants and flowers were everywhere. It almost looked like a secret garden. There were tinkling bells, and ropes of pearl, and gossamer fairies hung from invisible string. They seemed to fly through the air whenever there was any movement. Children's books were tenderly spread around the floor, but definitely not lined up on bookshelves.

Pearl and Jefferson had helped prepare the building for the grand opening. Now, Pearl stood inside as I opened the door. It seemed like hundreds of people, adults and children, were waiting.

"Ready, Mom?" I asked.

She nodded, took a deep breath, and stepped outside.

"We have waited a long time for this day, and it has been years since anything has happened here." Her voice got more confident and louder as she spoke. "So...welcome to The Persnickety Witch! We hope you'll come back again and again."

Her voice was clear and carried through the waiting crowd. She smiled, moved to the side, and allowed the excited people to pass her and enter the building. "Please, come in."

I encouraged children to find a seat on the magic mat for the story hour. Adults stood behind the fence, almost out of the confines of the porch. Clover stretched and yawned. Mist appeared from hidden places. Lights dimmed. Little eyes got big with anticipation. Then I began to tell a story with gusto and emotion and feeling.

"Thank you for coming to the grand opening of The Persnickety Witch. Did you know that everyone has a story? You do, and you, and even I do. I have a really good story to tell you today. Have you heard about…"